MW00936023

This is a work of fiction. Names, characters, places, and incidents are either the product of the author's imagination or are used fictitiously, and any resemblance to actual persons living or dead, business establishments, events, or locales, is entirely coincidental.

The Stealth Warrior: Navy SEAL Romance 2.0

Cover design: Steven Novak

Edited by Daniel Coleman, Valerie Bybee, and Shaleena Moy

Birch River Publishing

Smithfield, Utah

Published in the United States of America

THE STEALTH WARRIOR

Navy SEAL Romance 2.0

CAMI CHECKETTS

Birch River Publishing

FREE BOOK

Sign up for Cami's VIP newsletter and receive a free ebook copy of *The Resilient One: A Billionaire Bride Pact Romance* here.

You can also receive a free copy of *Rescued by Love: Park City Firefighter Romance* by clicking here and signing up for Cami's newsletter.

PROLOGUE

Kiera Richins clung to Creed Hawk's broad back. She could feel the perfect ridges of muscle through his t-shirt. He'd been home on leave from the SEALs for less than a week, and in the morning, he would leave her again. Why did it feel like this was truly goodbye instead of see you soon? She ached more than if she'd been en pointe for hours on end. Physical agony, she could handle. Losing Creed? Her world would shatter.

Creed pulled back slightly, and his dark gaze focused on her. The moonlight sparkled off of his handsome face. The waves rolled and gently crashed into the sand beneath their feet as they stood on the beach near his parents' Sands Point home on Long Island. Kiera hardly took notice of the saltwater drenching the hem of her floor-length sundress. All she could focus on was Creed, and all she could wish was he wasn't going to put his life on the line again. He was honorable and heroic, and she loved him for it, but why did it have to hurt so much to constantly be ripped apart from each other?

"It's all right, love," Creed said, understanding her unspoken worries. "Only four more months, and then my enlistment's up. Then you'll never have to say goodbye to this handsome face again."

She smiled, knowing his over-confidence was more to tease her, keep her from wallowing over his imminent departure. Creed didn't actually care that he was the best-looking man on the planet. He and his famous brothers had heard it often enough. Her smile fell away. "I don't want you to give up the SEALs for me. You live and breathe it." Though it was true, she hated saying those words. Hated trying to be brave when she felt anything but.

"I live and breathe you," he murmured, touching his warm lips to hers. Their mouths got caught up in an intricate dance that was better than any ballet or salsa move she could perform with her body. That was saying a lot since she'd been focused on mastering both disciplines from the day she started to walk. She sometimes wondered how Creed choreographed their kisses to be so all-encompassing, so perfect, but right now, she couldn't spend any time wondering, she simply let herself feel and savor.

Creed pulled back, but Kiera tugged him closer, running her hands over his shoulders and his broad back. "I want to be with you," she said quickly before she lost her nerve. She wanted to become one with him and know that they were bound together by something stronger than the promises they'd made. If she lost him, she wanted to have this memory, this night together. As her awkward words escaped, she knew all the saints in heaven were muttering prayers over her right now. Her staunchly Catholic abuelita would ring her neck if she was still around to curse and cuss Kiera like she had been wont to do.

"You are with me," Creed said.

Kiera gulped and didn't know if she could spell it out. She truly shouldn't spell it out, should just hug him and move on, but she couldn't resist him any longer. She needed the bonding of their love to sustain her when he left tomorrow.

"All the way with you," she whispered, guilt rushing in as quickly as the words escaped.

Creed's eyes widened, and then he studied her with a smoldering look that made fire rush through her. Kiera felt so alive yet terrified at the same time. They'd stayed strong for many years. One of them would always be sane enough to cool the fires before they raged out of control. What would the next step do to their relationship?

Creed's gaze swept over her, warm and filled with desire. Then he laughed. It wasn't a short, easy laugh. This laughter rumbled through his chest and blasted out of him. He laughed so hard he could hardly catch a breath.

Kiera gasped, pulled away from him, and folded her arms across her chest. "I'm glad my awkward offering could give you something to cackle about." She threw the words at him.

Creed stopped laughing though he was still smiling. "I know I'm irresistible, but did you *really* just proposition me?"

Kiera turned away, humiliated. "Don't think so highly of yourself, Creed Hawk. It was a once-in-a-lifetime offer that's gone now." She snapped her fingers at him.

Creed chuckled again, but then he sobered and turned her toward him, pulling her in tight. She didn't even attempt a resistance. "Sweet Kiera," he whispered huskily. "You have no clue how badly I want you, but remember our promise?"

Of course she remembered their promise. That promise had kept them from doing anything more than kissing for the past eight years, since he was a senior in high school and she was a sophomore. She'd fallen head over heels for Creed Hawk. They'd always been so in love it had been hard to stop their physical need for each other, but Creed was strong and disciplined, and so was she. They'd promised to save themselves for marriage and for each other, and though she loved their promise and had worked hard to honor it, she couldn't deny that she wanted more right now.

"It's still true, love. Our bond is stronger than a physical one, and when we're bound together before God, his angels, and all of our loved ones, being together will be magical for us." He kissed her softly and whispered against her lips, "I promise."

"But what if you don't come back to me?" She felt like a whiny little girl instead of the accomplished, renowned dancer she was. She was one of twenty dancers out of thousands of applicants to win a spot on *America's Got Talent: Just Dance*. She'd worked her entire life to be at the top. Right now, she didn't care about anything except Creed coming back to her, and if wishes could come true, never leaving her.

Creed smiled that irresistible smile of his. "You're the reason I will come back."

He held her tight. Her head rested in the crook of his neck like they'd been designed for each other. She clung to him and blinked the tears away. Creed was strong, brilliant, and determined. He would come back to her. Then they'd get married and be together. He'd promised. So why was her stomach rolling, and why were her palms clammy with a premonition that all their love and promises might be swept away faster than the next wave?

Several weeks had passed since Kiera had been in Creed's arms. She savored the memory every chance she got, but she'd also worked fourteen to sixteen-hour days getting ready for the chance of a lifetime—the finals of *America's Got Talent: Just Dance*. Miraculously, she and her partner, Milo, had won the competition. The moment was amazing, with her parents being there to celebrate and so many friends and family supporting her. Creed's parents had also been in the crowd, but sadly, Creed couldn't be there.

The celebration continued as she and Milo were interviewed on daytime shows. Offers to not only dance on the biggest stages in the world, but to be the focus of the show, started rolling in.

Soon, it was back to work, which Kiera actually preferred. She hadn't minded the interviews and the hype, but she'd worked long days for so many years to be where she was at, and she simply loved to dance, to move, and to improve her dancing. Milo was a well-matched partner for her. They'd worked together on Broadway before they'd taken the shot at *Just Dance*. Since it had paid off, they were spending a lot of time together. He was a nice guy and an amazing dancer, but Kiera had had to draw lines a few times and explain she'd already found the love of her life.

Someday, she and Creed would be together. That dream and her memories of Creed were a part of everything she did, giving her strength, direction, and hope.

Kiera and Milo were practicing in a rented studio for a show in London tonight. They finished an intimate bachata-style salsa number, and Milo ran his hand down her waistline, giving her a smoldering look. Kiera straightened and tried to move away, but Milo grasped her waist and pulled her in tight.

"The song's over," she said, hoping her voice sounded cold and unemotional.

"But you and I could just be starting," Milo whispered.

Kiera jerked free and folded her arms across her chest. "There is no us, Milo. I told you I have a boyfriend."

Milo stepped closer, his chest brushing her arms. "What kind of an idiot boyfriend can't even be there for the biggest events of your life?"

Kiera unfolded her arms and pushed hard at his chest. He instinctively stepped back. "You're the idiot. Don't ever come on to me again or we're done as partners."

Milo rolled his eyes and gave a disgusted grunt. "We're fabulous together, Kiera. You have to see that."

Kiera would lose a lot of contracts if she dumped him as a dance partner, but at the moment, she didn't care. Why did Creed have to be so far away? If he was here now, he'd whip Milo's butt, and the guy would never try anything like this again.

"We're fabulous as dance partners. That's all." She arched an eyebrow and dared him to challenge her. If he couldn't keep things platonic between them, she'd have to find another partner. The thought made her neck tighten. It would be a nightmare to find a partner with Milo's talent and dedication. On top of that was the fact they had won *Just Dance* as a couple. What would happen to all their contracts if they split up?

Milo spread his hands and lifted his shoulders. "You can't blame a guy for trying." He grinned at her.

"That's what you think." Kiera turned and strode to where she'd left her water bottle and purse by the edge of the wooden floor. "Let's take a break," she said.

Milo shrugged, clicked off the music, and headed for the bathroom.

Kiera took a long swallow of water, trying to calm her racing heart. Milo made her so mad, bagging on Creed like that, but she needed him if she was going to be successful in her career. Maybe it was time to keep her eyes open for another partner, quietly have her agent put out some feelers. This wasn't the first time Milo had made a pass at her, and she doubted it would be the last. She blew out a breath. Ah, Creed. Why did he have to be on some secretive mission? She missed him but at the same time, she was so proud of him. Creed had been born to succeed in the military, and he was on an elite team of SEALs now. She knew he was doing amazing things for their country, and it made her love him even more, no matter how badly she missed him.

She pulled her phone out of her purse to check her messages. The phone button showed seventeen missed calls. Kiera blinked. Nobody ever called her, except for her mama. Sure enough, all of the calls were from her mama. She pushed the call back button, her stomach dropping. What if something was wrong with her papa?

"Kiera!" Her mama's voice was mostly just a wail.

"Mama?" Kiera's heart beat faster and faster. "What's wrong?"

"Oh, mi amor. I wish I could hold you. Oh, mija."

"Mama! Please tell me what's going on." She could barely grip the phone.

"C-creed." Her mama gasped out. "Callum called. He thought I should be the one to tell you. The Navy just called Creed's dad."

Kiera felt the phone slipping from her grasp, but the words came through before she lost it, the words she never could accept. "Creed's dead."

CHAPTER ONE

Kiera did her bows, keeping the smile plastered on her face though inside she wanted to crumple. Tonight was her first performance since Creed had been killed a month ago. It had been more than obvious to everyone in the packed San Francisco theater that she was off. Clinging to Milo's hand, she waved with her other hand. The stage lights finally dimmed, and she was able to rip her hand free and run for her dressing room.

She ignored the whispers and stares. What did she care what anyone thought of her? Without Creed in this world, it was a struggle to want the sun to shine. She finally reached her dressing room and hurried inside. Before she could shut the door, a firm hand pushed it back open. Milo.

Kiera wanted to shove him out and just have a long, lonely cry, but how many tears could one person shed?

Milo ushered her into the room and quietly shut the door behind them. He gave her an understanding grimace and tugged her into his arms. Maybe Kiera should've resisted, but she was exhausted physically and more so emotionally. Milo had been there for her since Creed died, and except for all the times he'd tried before Creed's death to push her to give him a chance romantically, they were fantastic partners and friends.

"It's okay." Milo ushered her head to his chest. He was wiry, and women around the world fawned over him, but his build was nothing compared to Creed's. How could it be possible she would never feel Creed's arms around her again?

She let the tears flow for a few minutes, appreciating having something solid to cling to. Finally, she forced herself to straighten and pull back. "Thanks. Sorry I'm such a mess."

"Hey. Nobody is blaming you."

"I know, but I was so off tonight. Without you, that show would've been a total flop."

Milo raised one shoulder, taking her compliment with grace. "We all have off nights."

"Not like that." She walked to the leather couch and sank down into it. Milo followed her, sitting close. "Maybe I should just be done."

"No!" Milo's response was quick and intense. He turned and grasped her hands. "Kiera, you've worked too hard and too long. You have more talent than any dancer I've worked with. I need you."

Kiera studied him. She appreciated his words, but she couldn't fathom them. How could she simply move on from Creed's death and keep pursuing her dreams? She didn't want Milo or anyone to need her. She was barely functioning. How could she be needed by someone?

"What did Creed's letter tell you?"

Kiera swallowed hard and looked away. She'd received a letter shortly after Creed's death, and it had been beautiful and horrible at the same time. He was so full of love for her and kept begging her to move on from him, to live her life, be successful, be happy, to find love again. She loved the letter because it was as if Creed was talking to her from beyond the grave, but she hated to even think of moving on. It simply wasn't possible. How did you move on from the perfect man for you?

Milo was studying her, so she finally mumbled, "He wants me to be happy."

Milo nodded. "He was always so proud of you. Do this for him. Dance your heart out. Be happy. Find love again."

It was impossible to not notice how he squeezed her hand as he said the last sentence. Kiera's heart had no room to love again, but she felt Milo's words deeply. She could plunge herself back into dance, and though she doubted true happiness existed without Creed, she could be successful for him. That much she could do, and she knew Creed would be proud. Maybe someday, years in the future, happiness and love would come again, but for right now, she would focus on hard work and success, keep herself busy enough to hopefully dull the pain.

"I'll work hard for him," she said, the mere words giving her strength. "I can do that ... for Creed."

Milo grinned and rubbed his thumb along the back of her hand. "That's my girl."

She was not his girl and never would be, but she had no energy to debate anything right now.

"We'll do it together," Milo said. He released her hand and wrapped his arm around her shoulder. "I'll never leave your side."

Kiera thought that was a little dramatic, but she couldn't deny she needed his encouragement and friendship right now. She let herself lean against his shoulder, and she kept repeating one thing in her mind: "For Creed. For Creed."

CHAPTER TWO

Kiera could not do this tonight. She stormed out of the fancy dressing room in the Bellagio and into the wide hall with the obnoxious carpet and walls that were papered with fake gold accents. Other performers milled around or rushed by to get ready for the performance. She should be focused mentally on her upcoming performance, but she had to get away from Milo and his constant attention. Milo had been respectful and stayed by her side since Creed died three months ago, playing the part of loyal friend. Unfortunately, the façade hadn't lasted near long enough for her. A few weeks ago, he'd started putting on the moves again, sometimes showing up at her condo door early in the morning or ridiculously late at night. She had to constantly tell him sorry but no. She appreciated and liked the guy, and they were perfect as dance partners. She clung to the words in Creed's letter about finding happiness and being successful, but she couldn't imagine ever moving on to another man. No matter how sneakily Milo tried to pretend that they had a relationship deeper than dancing partners, she didn't know if she would ever be ready for that.

There was a loud disturbance and sounds of fighting down the hall. She turned to look, but Milo was suddenly there. He grabbed her and pulled her in, smothering her with his hot lips. Kiera stood absolutely still. She felt angry. Well, at least it was some emotion. Since Creed had died she'd felt absolutely nothing, except for the desire to succeed for him. The hard work and long hours had been exactly what she needed to keep getting out of bed each morning. She was glad she had a purpose. If only she could keep Milo at a distance. She'd heard he and his agent were pushing for him and Kiera to have a romantic relationship. She knew the media was having a heyday speculating about their status and what a great couple they would make.

Milo finally stopped pushing a kiss that she wasn't returning and simply held her close.

She heard her name being screamed, and the voice almost sounded like ... Creed. Now, she was definitely going crazy. She thought she'd retained her sanity these past months as she worked nonstop and only sobbed for Creed late at night. Clearly, she was wearing down. Even succeeding for the love of her life had lost its appeal. She didn't know how much longer she could keep up the celebrity lifestyle. She'd recently talked to her agent about doing an international tour or going back to Broadway. The work would be demanding but not as high profile as television and stage shows featuring her and Milo. The other benefit was she could get away from Milo. Being on her own sounded very appealing right now.

She turned to look at the man who had yelled for her, but all she could see was two security guards with some guy pinned down.

Milo hurried her back into her dressing room, shut the door, and locked it. He smiled possessively at her. "There are too many crazies who want you." He took a step closer, and she backed up. "Lucky for me, I'm the one who's got you."

She put a hand on his chest. "We need to talk." She was fired up about all the rumors of her and Milo. The latest was that he'd moved in with her and the pictures of him leaving her condo at all hours were exactly what the media needed to feed those rumors. Though Milo didn't seem to be getting the message, she had explained very carefully that she would never sleep with him before marriage, and she'd also explained that her heart had been gouged out when Creed, the only man she'd ever truly loved, had been killed three months ago.

She had no heart left to give, and though she didn't mind being around Milo, sans rumors of living with him and having to repeatedly turn him down, she felt nothing but friendship for him. Him trying to kiss her had been pathetic and empty.

Her phone rang, and she ignored it.

Milo walked past her and picked it up, extending it to her. "It's your mother, sweetheart."

She could see it in his eyes. He knew she was done with their shallow relationship, and he wanted to put off "the talk" as long as possible. She was pretty sure he or his agent were the ones instigating the rumors. The media twisted a lot of things, but why would they make up her and Milo living together and a story about him buying a huge engagement ring. The thought of either made her stomach squeamish.

She took the phone from his outstretched palm. "Hola, Mama." Her mama was from Spain and her papa from Nigeria. They'd met at NYU and settled in America after they fell in love.

"Mi amor. Have you heard? Have you heard?"

"Heard what Mama?"

Milo was studying her, and she gave him a fake smile and turned away.

"Creed is alive! Oh mija, mi querida. Creed's alive!"

Kiera's entire body seemed to freeze. The room started spinning and then everything went black.

Creed Hawk couldn't run fast enough along the busy sidewalk and up the ramp toward the massive Bellagio resort, dodging tourists and high-dollar escorts. He ignored the crowds, the water shows, the dry heat, and the filth that was Vegas. Four months without Kiera. Three months of everyone he loved believing he was dead. He'd spent the last two days being debriefed, interrogated, de-bugged, de-wormed, fed, and showered. Then he was finally allowed to travel home to see his family. Some English chap had gotten into their barracks before they'd disbanded and asked SEAL Team 2 to work for him. Creed thought it sounded great and had said he was in, but he needed a few days to see his family and Kiera and figure out what he wanted in his future. He didn't need money, but working undercover with the other former SEALs, righting wrongs and protecting the innocent, definitely held an appeal. He'd be like Batman, only better-looking and buffer. As long as it didn't interfere with time with Kiera. She was his future now.

Last night, he had finally made it home to Long Island and got to simply sit and hold his mom close. When her sobs slowed to sniffles and he was able to disengage without too much guilt from her desperate clasp, he shared manly hugs with Callum,

Bridger, Emmett, and his dad and was introduced to Emmett's new fiancée, Cambree. He got a kick out of Cambree, she had no filter and was funny and obviously in love with his brother.

After they talked into the early morning, his mom never leaving his side, he explained to his family he needed to fly to Vegas the next day and find Kiera. He'd written her a Dear Jane letter that was only supposed to be delivered if he died. He'd died, but he'd come back, and now, he was finally free to find Kiera. To marry her and be with her like they'd always dreamed. Maybe he should've called her as soon as he'd been allowed to, but he needed to see her in person, explain that the Dear Jane letter encouraging her to find happiness and move on with her life was only written because of how much he loved her. All he needed now was to hold her close.

He grinned as he saw a huge banner of his beautiful girlfriend splayed across a walkway, ignoring the blond man also in the picture. Milo was only her dance partner. Creed didn't like any man putting their clammy hands on his girl, but he could respect that was part of her career and knew Kiera was a complete professional.

He focused on her gorgeous face. She was the most perfect mix of her tall Nigerian papa and her petite Spaniard mama. He'd never seen a more exquisite woman than Kiera. She had won *America's Got Talent: Just Dance* the week before he'd gone on the mission that had ended in three months of misery and torture. She was amazing. From what he understood, she was in high demand performing across the world. He was proud of her and couldn't wait to watch her perform and cheer obnoxiously. But right now, he simply needed to hold her. Nothing would be right until she was in his arms.

He followed the signs to the O Theater where she would be

performing tonight. He had half an hour until the show. Just enough time to hold her and kiss her and let her see he'd survived for her, just like he told her he would.

He skirted the theater and found the backstage entrance that Blaine had helped him scope out. Creed had studied the blueprints on his taxi ride from the airport. Blaine was big on never taking Uber or Lyft because then someone could track your information. Creed teased him about it, but he also followed the advice.

Two well-built security guards in suits with obvious earpieces stood in front of him, blocking his access to the performers. There was a long hallway behind them with lots of doors and people in sparkly costumes rushing in and out.

"Hey, how are ya?" He tried for laidback Western appeal when what he wanted was to take them both out and sprint for Kiera. "I'm meeting up with Kiera Richins before the show."

The taller guy grunted. "Yeah, right. Don't we all wish we could 'meet up with Kiera Richins.'"

His bald partner nodded. "Get lost, dude."

Creed's gut tightened. Okay, so he'd have to take them both out. Not that he minded a good fist fight, but he didn't want to get in the middle of a security issue while he could be holding Kiera. He should've taken that Sutton guy up on his offer to get him into Kiera's dressing room, but he'd wanted to do this on his own. Sutton had acted a little awkward about him needing to see Kiera in person to tell her he was alive when Creed had explained the situation in Syria. Creed brushed it off. Not many people could understand the depth of his and Kiera's relationship.

"Yeah, here's the thing." Creed dodged at the taller one first, getting in a quick uppercut to the abdomen and a jab to the ribs before he felt the big baldy coming. He popped his elbow back and connected with the guy's jaw. Creed put the first guy in a headlock and turned and jammed tall guy's head into baldy's abdomen.

People down the hall were crying out in dismay. Creed glanced up, and suddenly, there she was. Kiera stormed out of an open doorway, not even glancing his way. The graceful beauty of her movements, her perfectly-proportioned face, and the long, dark hair trailing down her back knocked Creed's breath from his body. His memories of her didn't do her justice.

A tall blond guy followed her out of the door, grabbed her, whirled her around and pulled her in tight. He kissed her like he owned the right to her lips. Creed cried out and his arms went slack. The guy he was holding slipped out of his grasp and the baldy tackled Creed to the ground. The tall guy added his weight, and they both pinned him down.

Creed looked up, and Kiera was still in the blond idiot's arms. They weren't kissing, but he was clinging to her, and she hadn't even glanced in Creed's direction.

"Kiera," Creed hollered. She pulled back and turned his way, but the two guys dog-piled him. One of them repeatedly smacked him in the back of the head, and he couldn't see her. With a roar, he threw them off, but Kiera and the blond man were gone. Kiera. And that loser Milo. She hadn't resisted the guy. She hadn't slapped him. All the fight went out of Creed.

The guys wrestled him back to the ground, and he didn't even resist. He laid on the industrial carpet. The weight of the two men on top of him didn't hurt nearly as much as his dreams going up in smoke. Kiera was with someone else? His brain couldn't process it, but his heart was aching enough for his entire body.

Four more security guards appeared, and they all worked together, ripping him to his feet and hauling him off. Creed just stared down the hallway where he'd seen his dream woman being kissed and hugged by another man, not even responding to his call for her. He'd survived months of torture for this?

Kiera opened her eyes to Milo standing over her, grasping his cell phone. "She's coming around now," he said then dropped to his knees. "Are you okay? Kiera? The paramedics will be here any second."

Kiera pushed past him and stood. "Paramedics? I don't need paramedics. Creed's alive!"

"Creed Hawk?" Milo's brow furrowed, and his blue eyes darkened. "That's not possible." He shook his head at her, all sad and understanding. "I'm sorry, precious. I know it's been hard, but you have to accept the truth. Creed's gone, but I'm here for you."

"Argh!" She half-grunted, half-yelled at him. "My mama wouldn't lie to me." She searched the floor and found her phone, pressing it to her ear and ignoring Milo. "Mama, are you there?"

"Are you all right?"

"I passed out I think. Oh, mama, he's really alive?"

"Si, mi amor. Are you coming home?"

"Yes! I'll call you as soon as I know the details."

"I'll pick you up at the airport and drive you straight to Creed. Oh, I'm so happy!"

"Me too!" Kiera ran past Milo and grabbed her purse, ending the call and stuffing her phone in it. She wished she had time to change out of her white sequined stage costume, but nothing could keep her from Creed.

She hurried to the door, but Milo grasped her arm. "What are you doing? Where are you going?"

"I'm going to New York. Creed's alive!" Her heart threatened to burst. The Dear Jane letter Creed had sent telling her to move on meant nothing now. She and Creed were meant to be together, and he was alive. She didn't know such happiness could exist after the past three months of misery. She couldn't stop grinning.

"We've got a show in twenty minutes, and what about us?"

"They'll have to cancel the show, and I'm sorry, but there is no us." Kiera ripped her arm free and ran for the door. By tomorrow morning, she'd be in Creed's arms.

Two hours after Creed's dreams had been smashed and tattered, Sutton Smith, the British guy who looked like James Bond, walked into the security office. Creed was properly cuffed and not even fighting. He always fought. It was who he was. A hot head and a smart aleck and the man who loved Kiera. But did she love somebody else? Had his alleged death driven her into another man's arms and driven Creed out of her heart?

Sutton smirked at Creed and sat across from him. "Are you ready to stop wallowing and get to work?"

Stop wallowing? It had been two lousy hours since his world had fallen apart. He was entitled to a little indulgent misery. "Is she dating that guy?" Creed demanded. Somehow he knew Sutton had all the answers, and suddenly, he also knew why Sutton had acted so off in Syria about him finding Kiera.

"Milo Lopez—a B-list actor, acclaimed Broadway star, and Kiera's dance partner."

Creed glared. He didn't need the guy's credentials. He needed to know what he was doing with Creed's girl and how Creed could rip them apart.

"For the past few months, they've been inseparable." Sutton paused and eyed him, as if concerned how he would take his next words. "Even before your mission."

"She's his dance partner." Creed exploded. Surely a man as accomplished as Sutton Smith understood the difference between performing and real relationships. Yes, Milo and Kiera worked closely together, but Kiera would never cross those emotional and physical lines.

Even if you were dead and told her to go be happy, to live her life? A snide voice whispered in his head.

Creed's jaw tightened. No. Not Kiera. Not in three stinking months.

Sutton gave him an understanding look. "I'm afraid it's more than that. Of course the press have been claiming Milo and Kiera are together but I took the liberty of asking Logan to dig."

If Logan found the information, Creed could trust it. But what if that information confirmed the unwanted compassion in Sutton's eyes?

Sutton threw some pictures on the table. Creed forced himself to glance over them. He could hardly stomach the ones of Kiera in Milo's arms. None of them were of them kissing but he'd seen that with his own eyes. With his hands cuffed he couldn't rip the evidence of Kiera and Milo being together outside of dancing to shreds.

Sutton pointed to several shots of Milo walking out of a

ritzy-looking high-rise. "Kiera's condo. Some of these are early in the morning, some extremely late at night."

Creed's chest tightened.

"His agent confirmed to Logan that Milo Lopez moved in with her three weeks ago, and he recently purchased a five-karat diamond ring."

Creed dropped his chin to his chest. He felt like his insides were being ripped apart, but he'd been trained to project no emotion. Three lousy months he'd been dead, and Kiera had moved on that easily? Found somebody else. Living with him? The Kiera he'd known and loved would never live with someone. She was a strong Christian, and they'd both committed to saving themselves for marriage ... to each other. Their last night together, she'd offered herself to him, but that was because she loved him so much. She wouldn't do that with another man, would she?

His heart felt like it had splintered inside of him. Had celebrity status changed Kiera? Was she no longer the woman he craved and could never be without? He loved her more than anything in the world. And right now, he hated this Milo joker and the images of the guy holding her more than anything in the world.

All those years, all those promises. They'd stayed pure for each other. Even when it was tougher than sitting in a sweltering cave in Afghanistan and not moving for hours. Staying strong while kissing Kiera had been much harder than that. And she threw all their love and discipline away on some B-list actor. Rage filled his chest, and he felt like he was under water. Like during BUDs training when they would have to lay in the sand and do scissor kicks on their backs as the waves rolled over them. He would hold his breath until the wave receded, but sometimes he was completely out of oxygen and his abs were screaming for relief. He would pull in air too soon, and then he would be suffocating, certain he was going to die. That's what this felt like.

He finally raised his eyes. Sutton's blue eyes were serious, understanding, like someone who'd been there. Creed didn't need his sympathy. He needed to escape from the reality of a world where Kiera didn't love him enough to wait. A world where his girl gave her purity and love to someone else, without even waiting to marry the loser. Would Kiera really do that? He'd told her in his letter to be happy, to move on, but not like this. Their love felt cheapened and disgusting now. She'd thrown away their love like an already-used gun casing, not even worth finding a trash can for. His stomach churned, and his mouth filled with bile.

"Do you have underground assignments?" he asked.

Sutton quirked an eyebrow.

"I want to be in the dark to *anything* that happens in America."

Sutton nodded his understanding. "I'll give you the darkest assignments I can find and make sure everyone knows you want no reports on American social media."

Darkness, tough assignments, and a world where Kiera and Milo didn't exist sounded like the best option available to him. "When do I start?" he muttered.

Sutton gave him half a smile. "I thought you would never ask. Welcome aboard, young chap."

CHAPTER THREE

The ride to the airport, waiting until after midnight to pay an exorbitant amount to get on a plane, being in the air on a red-eye flight for six hours and forty-two minutes, none of it could wipe the perma-grin off Kiera's face. Even though time passed excruciatingly slowly and she got some strange looks in her stage costume and makeup—until the people recognized her and interrupted her daydreams of Creed asking for autographs—her happiness didn't evaporate as her mind kept repeating over and over again "*Creed's alive. Creed's alive*!"

She couldn't wait to be in his arms. They'd fallen in love in high school. He and his brothers were all superhero athletes, handsome and sought after by every girl whose hormones worked properly. Creed had been the quarterback for Paul D. Schreiber High School, and his brother Emmett was their wide receiver. The two broke every record at the school then went on to play college ball together at Cornell. Emmett went on to play professionally for the Titans, but Creed enrolled in Navy training during college, like they all knew he would. He was determined to make a difference, and he would rather be below the water than on land.

When Kiera had first seen Creed, she'd been a sophomore and he was a senior. His family was from the unreal expensive area of Sands Point, whereas her parents were middle class and had a condo in Manorhaven, which was considered the most dangerous neighborhood in Port Washington, Long Island. Kiera smiled. Dangerous was a relative term. She loved all of Long Island and had always felt safe. The fact that the billionaire hunk Creed Hawk had noticed her still shocked her. His friends and brothers gave him a hard time about robbing the cradle, but Creed didn't care. He only had eyes for Kiera, and she'd been enamored with him from day one as well.

So much history together and so much love. Then he'd died. She shuddered. All that awful emptiness and sadness was behind her now. Creed was alive.

She finally made it onto land, through the airport, and into her mama's arms. When her mama could see through the tears, they jumped into her Volvo, and her mama drove like a crazy woman through the morning rush hour toward Creed's parents' colonial mansion on Sands Point. When Kiera stumbled out of her mama's old car at the Hawk mansion gate, she knew she was a mess—wearing her costume outfit and makeup, some of her makeup smeared from the tears of happiness she couldn't stop crying. She wanted to yell to everyone—Creed's alive!

"Ma'am?" the guard said respectfully but warily.

"Creed." She gushed out. "I'm here for Creed." She clasped her hands together and couldn't stop grinning. "Kiera Richins. I'm his girlfriend."

The guard glanced over her sequined white dress with the

high thigh slit so she could move easily. His glance said he wondered if she was a crazed Hawk brothers' fan. She prayed he wouldn't call the cops on her. Dredging up every bit of training, she tilted her chin and gave him a challenging look.

Recognition flared in his eyes. "You're the *Just Dance* lady," he murmured.

At least he'd recognized her and probably wouldn't throw her out. "I need to see Creed ... please."

He nodded. "Just a moment, ma'am." He paced away from her and pulled out his phone, conferring for far too long. Finally, he pushed open the walking gate and ushered her through. "Do you need assistance to the house?" he asked, glancing down at her high-heeled dancing shoes.

She laughed. "I can sprint in these things." And sprint she did, feeling so carefree and happy. She was here. Creed was here. Life was beautiful and wonderful. Running along the wooded path that paralleled the tree-lined drive, Kiera finally spotted the huge Colonial mansion. Kiera had always loved this spacious house with the wide planks, black shutters, huge porch, and the views over the sweeping lawn, pool area, and the ocean beyond. But it was the love that filled the house that made her so happy. Creed's mom was an angel, and his brothers were very similar in dark good looks but very different in personality, talents, and temperament. Despite that, they were all good men who could tease her like a sister.

The front door sprang open as she crossed the circle drive and raced past the water features. Caroline ran out with her arms wide. She was a few inches shorter than Kiera's five six and was always done up to the nines with her dark hair perfectly coiffed and in a different color of business suit and skirt every day. Yet she'd bake cookies and cuddle and wrestle with her boys as if she was in holey sweats. Kiera loved her almost as much as she loved her own mama.

"Beautiful girl, you're here!"

Kiera pumped her way up the stairs as Caroline descended them. They slammed so hard into each other Kiera would've lost her balance if she hadn't been born with the ability to teeter on her toes for hours. Caroline held her tight. Tears ran unchecked down Kiera's face. A small part of her wished she could clean off her stage makeup that had to be smeared to kingdom come and get all beautiful for Creed, but most of her couldn't care less. She just wanted his arms around her and knew he would feel the same, no matter what his letter said about her moving on with her life, no matter how many horrors he must've gone through being imprisoned for three months. They were meant to be together and heal each other's hurts. Creed would want her even with the makeup smears.

"He's alive." Caroline kept repeating it. "I'm just so happy."

"I want him!" It came out as an anguished wail, and the words sounded completely inappropriate to say to Creed's mother, but she knew Caroline would understand. Kiera had distanced herself from the Hawks because of how hard it had been to see each other and be reminded of losing Creed all over again, ripping the unhealed wound open over and over again. Still, she knew the Hawks loved her, and she loved them. Her heart was bursting with happiness. They could all be one big happy family again. Creed would come soon—hold her, kiss her. They could start making plans for when they would get married. She knew he'd support her in her career, but that was the last thing on her mind right now. She needed Creed more than water, food, or air. More than dancing. Okay, she was getting a little dramatic, but she loved him so much.

"Oh, sweetheart." Caroline pulled back and daintily swiped her tears away with her first finger. "You just missed him. He ... had to leave."

"Leave? Where?" Surely, she'd heard wrong. Creed would never *leave*. He'd know Kiera would come. In fact, if he had the time, the Creed she missed and loved would've flown straight to find her. She knew it.

"Packed up his stuff and left with some charming English man an hour ago."

Caroline's words screeched all of Kiera's dreams to a halt. Caroline studied her like she might break apart. With good cause. Creed had *left*?

"Did he go looking for me?" She clenched her hands together, terrified of the answer. She never thought she'd be terrified of anything Creed would do. What was happening?

"Earlier I thought he was going to." Caroline seemed as confused as Kiera felt. "You didn't see him in Vegas?"

Kiera shook her head.

"I was so certain he was going to find you, but now he's headed to California."

California? If Creed really went to Vegas, why didn't he find her? In the hallway, after Milo kissed her, she thought she'd heard Creed's voice call her name. If that had been Creed he wouldn't have left without finding her. She was so confused.

"When's he coming back?" she asked in a small, unsteady voice. She would wait. Though it hurt that he hadn't been able to wait for her, what was a few more days when they were going to be together forever? He must've had to go on an essential assignment. Surely there was someone dying who needed Creed's skills and help. That was the only reason he'd leave before he saw her. She had to believe that or she would crumble.

"I don't know exactly how long, sweetheart."

"Can we call him?"

Caroline wrapped her hand around Kiera's arm as if in a show of support. "He ... he said there's no way for us to get a hold of him. Said he'll be 'underground' for"—Caroline swallowed—"months." She looked down as if she couldn't meet Kiera's gaze. "He asked me to send his things to California."

Kiera stared, not even blinking. Most of all not comprehending. Was Caroline trying to say that Creed had been brought back from the dead, only to leave her again?

"The job is undercover and very important. Somebody needs him. You know Creed." Caroline smiled, but it fell away quickly.

Kiera did know Creed. Knew and loved him completely. He'd been her world. She'd been proud and thought it was very honorable when he'd enlisted in the Navy then worked his way into being a SEAL and then on a special elite task force. Her stomach rolled. All of Creed's accomplishments made her suddenly ill. She'd assumed he'd done everything because of his love for America which he'd claimed was deeper because of his love for Kiera. It had been hard when he'd missed the entire season of *America's Got Talent: Just Dance*. Especially when she won and he couldn't be there to pick her off her feet and kiss her in that joyful moment. She had expected to make sacrifices as the loved one of a Navy SEAL, and she'd never begrudged him serving his country. Yet now, when he should have returned to her, he'd chosen an undercover job over her? He was so noble and good, and of course, someone needed him, but why couldn't that someone be her?

She was numb. Creed hadn't cared enough to even come find her before he left again? He'd been resurrected from death, and he couldn't even send her a text? Maybe she could understand if he would've at least made an effort. Would it have killed him to call? Explain why he had to leave?

"Come inside, sweetheart. You look exhausted."

Kiera pulled back and shook her head. She wasn't exhausted. She was heartbroken and shattered, and as the depth of Creed's rejection and betrayal sunk in, she was royally ticked off. She focused in on Caroline. Creed's mom didn't deserve Kiera's wrath. Creed did. "I ... I'd better go be with my mama and"—she gestured to her ridiculous outfit—"change out of this."

Caroline nodded, pretending she understood, pretending they didn't both know that Creed apparently didn't love Kiera enough to make any effort to contact her. Ditched. She'd been ditched by the man who was her world. What kind of man did that to the woman he claimed to love? Not her Creed. Had his imprisonment changed him, stripped him of his ability to love her? In his letter he'd asked her repeatedly to move on, to find happiness and love. Had he planned even then to never come back to her? Maybe, before he'd been imprisoned, he'd already doubted their relationship? Doubted their love? The bottom fell out of her stomach. She was on an emotional roller coaster more vicious than any ride at Six Flags.

"I'll tell Creed I saw you when he calls."

"No!" Kiera shook her head fiercely. "Please don't, Caroline."

"But Kiera—"

"Please." Kiera swallowed hard so she wouldn't cry again. Before, the tears she'd been crying were due to happiness and anticipation and joy. Now, they would be bitter and selfish and pitiful. Kiera touched Caroline's arm. "If he didn't want to see me ..." She swallowed again and shook her head then bit her lip before taking a quick breath. Nothing helped, the tears spilled out.

"Oh, sweetheart, of course he wanted to see you!" Caroline crossed the distance between them and hugged her tight. "He's always loved you. It's always been you for Creed."

"Then why wouldn't he come for me? Why wouldn't he wait?" The anguished words rushed out, and Kiera wished she could call them back. She didn't want to do this with Creed's mom. It wasn't fair of her. This sweet woman had been through more than enough. Creed had left her too. How could he just leave his mom for some job, days after returning to her? This job must be singularly important. Unfortunately, that thought didn't help ease the pain at all.

"I don't know. But I know how much he loved you."

Kiera pulled back and studied Caroline's beautiful face. She had some laugh wrinkles around her mouth and eyes, which made her even more lovely. "Loved." She sniffed and nodded. "Something must have changed. He doesn't want me anymore." Was it possible that letter that she'd clung to and used as motivation to work hard and be successful was really Creed dumping her? He'd never planned to come back to her, even if he survived the imprisonment? He'd told her goodbye in that final letter, and she'd taken it as encouragement and love.

The world was crashing around her, and she could hardly stand up straight from the weight of it.

"No. I can't believe that," Caroline said. "He loves you."

"Then why would he leave without finding me? Not even a phone call, a text, an email. Nothing!"

Caroline blinked up at her. She shrugged her delicate shoulders. "There has to be some explanation."

Kiera didn't want to ask but she had to. "Did he even say anything? Did he even care?"

"Well of course he cared! He flew to Vegas."

"To find me?" She challenged. He sure hadn't found her. Even if that had been him in the hallway, he hadn't come for her. He'd flown back home and went straight to California. Why?

"Of course! At least, we all assumed so. I mean it was a whirlwind with hugging him and all of us asking so many questions, and then he hadn't met Emmett's fiancée, Cambree, so he wanted to get to know her. Anyway, late the first night he was home, he came and told us he was going to rush to Vegas the next morning and then he would be back. Of course that meant to find you."

"Did it?" She shook her head. "I never saw him. What did he say when he came back? He never said he was coming for me, did he?"

Caroline couldn't meet her gaze. "He didn't say anything. Just came late last night with that beautiful man with the English accent. Tom and the man chatted while I helped Creed pack. Creed was pretty somber, but I talked enough for the both of us, and then he was gone."

"He said nothing about seeing me?"

"I tried to ask him about you, if he saw you. He wouldn't talk about it. He seemed broken."

Kiera felt broken. The thought of Creed hurting and her not being able to fix him, be there for him, seared even more wounds open inside of her. She felt pain that he wouldn't let her fix him and hurt that she would never get the chance. She hadn't let herself think about his imprisonment too much, but did it break him, break their love or had his love for her disappeared before that?

There were so many questions and no answers. The only person who had those answers hadn't found her, if he'd even tried. It didn't seem like he'd made much of an effort, and now, she couldn't even call him and tell him off and then tell him she loved him. Tell him their love could surpass any pain, if only he would allow it to.

She backed away. One-sided love wouldn't be enough to fix anything, especially a man as strong and brave as Creed. If he didn't need her, she refused to be the wilting flower begging for a sip of water from him.

"Please don't tell him I came."

"But sweetheart ..." Caroline began.

"Please!" Kiera wasn't above begging. "I can't imagine what he's gone through, how hard it's been. Please don't burden him with this as well. It's obvious he doesn't want me anymore." Her voice broke. "Please promise me."

Caroline finally nodded, and she didn't reach for her this time. Right now, Kiera really needed that hug. "I'm so sorry, sweetheart."

"Not your fault." Kiera tried to be brave. "Thank you for always being so wonderful to me."

Caroline did hug her then. "It's going to work out. He'll find you," she whispered in her ear.

Kiera wished she could believe that. Creed was an impressive and stealthy tracker, but he couldn't find her if he didn't look.

She forced a smile and turned, walking slowly past the lovely fountains and cobblestone circle drive, along the path that she'd run down with such joyful abandon not long ago. Creed had come back. He was alive. She loved him desperately. And he didn't care enough to even call her.

Crazily, there were no tears left. Her heart was cold and empty. The pain that wracked her body made her want to vomit. It was like he'd died all over again. No, it was worse. At least when he'd died last time, others had shared in her grief, and she had that letter, so full of his love and his wishes for her to be happy. At least, she had thought that's what the letter meant.

She was horribly selfish to even have these thoughts. His mother and family had Creed back in their lives, and that was wonderful for them. But Kiera had nothing.

CHAPTER FOUR

Kiera spent the day with her mom and the evening with both of her parents, but she couldn't handle being in Long Island, so close to all those memories of Creed and unable to accept that it was truly over between them. That he'd moved on, dumping her and their love that easily.

She did the walk, or rather flight, of shame back to Las Vegas and her career. A quick text sent, and Milo met her at the airport with open arms. She heard some clicks and looked around to see they'd been recognized and several teenage girls were taking pictures. She couldn't even force a smile. Milo tried to start a conversation as they left the airport, but she wasn't quite ready to face him yet.

She motioned to the Uber driver. "Can we please just get to the studio and then talk?" she asked.

Milo nodded, keeping his arm around her. They finally arrived at the dance studio where they'd trained since being in Vegas. They went to their private workspace, a beautiful room that was all windows, mirrors, and hardwood floors. Milo shut the door and said, "I've been pretty patient Kiera. You cost us both hundreds of thousands of dollars, not to mention the bad publicity, missing that show. I need some answers."

Kiera acknowledged the truth of his statements with a nod. She swallowed and said, "I'm sorry I ran out on you. You have been a wonderful partner and friend, and you didn't deserve that."

Milo waited for more, but she didn't know quite how to explain. Truthfully, she didn't want to explain anything about Creed.

"So Creed's alive?"

Kiera couldn't hold his gaze. "Yes."

"But you're back here with me?"

Kiera drew in a deep breath and held it. When she thought her lungs would explode, she pushed out the words. "He doesn't want me."

There was silence for far too long. She forced herself to stand straight and meet Milo's gaze. Milo's eyes were soft and filled with more emotion than she wanted to deal with. "He's an idiot," he muttered.

Kiera took the words like a punch in the gut. Creed might be the biggest idiot on the planet to turn his back on what they'd had, but she didn't want to hear about it from Milo.

"Well, it's over, and now, I just want to get back to work," she said.

Milo shook his head. "I know it hurts, Kiera, but you have to know I'll always be here for you."

Kiera was bone tired, but she had to address this issue now. "You're the best dance partner anyone could ask for, but if I haven't made it clear before now, I need to. I don't feel anything more than friendship for you."

Milo's blue eyes darkened. "You've never given me a chance."

Kiera splayed her hands. "It's one of those things you just know Milo. There are no sparks between us, and our values are very different."

"I have been more patient with you than any man would dream of being."

Kiera thought that might be true. Two days ago, she would've argued that Creed would wait for her for an eternity, but apparently, that was false.

"We can still dance together," Kiera said, but even as she said it, she knew everything was imploding. She was too broken to keep fighting to be on top, to keep performing, to keep working with Milo and yet keep him at arm's length.

"I deserve better than your scraps," Milo yelled at her. "Tell me that you'll give us a chance or I am done!"

Kiera shook her head. "There will never be an us."

"I'm through." He pushed out a disgusted grunt then stormed past her to the door. Kiera whirled to watch him leave.

Milo turned, and his glower was so ugly it was hard to believe he was the same compassionate man of minutes before. "I will ruin you Kiera. You'll never dance in America again."

Kiera leaned away from the very solid threat he'd just thrown at her. Milo was a big star, but she was the one people raved about. Still, it would be all too easy for him to ruin her. Staying at the top of this game was a precarious dance, and it would be simple to topple off the peak at any time. She didn't know if she could continue the balancing act any longer.

Milo waited for her response, but her fire, her drive, had been killed by Creed's desertion. She'd survived these past three months, worked and thrived in her career, for Creed. No more. The weariness she'd been fighting since Creed had been pronounced dead overtook her. His death had about taken her under, but strangely, it was him coming back to life and not wanting her that threw the flowers on top of her coffin.

It was a struggle to stay on her feet. She couldn't find it in her to care if Milo ruined her or ran her name through the mud.

When she didn't respond, he simply sneered and stormed away. Kiera had no energy to get in the middle of some mud-slinging battle, and suddenly, the only thing she wanted was to get away from it all.

She leaned against the mirror, slipped her phone out of her purse, and dialed her agent's number. "I need two things."

"Name them." Ilene sang the words. She was the most upbeat person Kiera knew.

"I want a statement issued right now that I've split ways with Milo and we will not be performing in any upcoming shows."

Ilene gasped, but Kiera wasn't done. "And I want you to set up a tour for me. I want to be anywhere but America. I'll teach dance lessons at resorts in Cabo or do benefit shows for children in Africa. I'd prefer the last, but I honestly don't care. Just please get me away from here."

"What ... what happened?" Ilene asked.

"Just do this for me, please."

Silence came for a few beats. Then Ilene muttered, "If you're certain."

"I am."

"Then it's done."

It was done. She'd given up her hard-earned career, but at the moment, she couldn't find it in her to care. Creed had given up on her. Nothing could be more devastating than that.

CHAPTER FIVE

Two months later

Creed had settled into his room at the all-inclusive Cancun resort and was pretending he was like any other tourist who'd just arrived at the sprawling getaway. The massive buildings formed a wide u shape. The pools, restaurants, fitness center, and spa were nestled in the open middle of the buildings, with the beach and ocean visible beyond them. There were twelve sections of rooms with almost two hundred suites in each section. The place was like a gigantic cruise ship on land. Kiera had always wanted to go on a cruise. He rolled his eyes. Not thinking about Kiera.

He wandered through the buffet and tried a few things. He walked the length of the private beach and watched families playing volleyball, digging in the sand, snorkeling in the ocean, kayaking, or paddle-boarding. He checked out all eight of the massive pools, lost track of the number of hot tubs, and took a tour of the exclusive spa and well-equipped workout area. Of course, he also looked at the menus of each of the six restaurants.

To anyone watching, he appeared to be a tourist excited for vacation at the luxurious five-star resort, but he was far from it. Vacation and happiness held no appeal since he'd seen Kiera kissing Milo. He was on a job for Sutton Smith, and that meant being as vigilant as he'd ever been in the Navy. Sutton was a good man, but he didn't tolerate mistakes, and this job may be the most important of Creed's assignments thus far. Creed was stalking James Gunthry, former Duke of Gunthry, ex-husband of Sutton's lovely new wife Liz, and all-around slime ball. Creed had followed a trail through the Caribbean that had led him to Cancun and this very resort. After the duke had escaped during a prison transfer with the help of two well-paid guards, he had altered his appearance, going from dark hair to blond. He had added contact lenses that made his eyes green and had done botox to appear younger. He'd even gotten a new nose, more regal than his last one. He'd also put on twenty pounds of muscle, changing from weaselly to having a little bit of a build. However, Creed could, and would, still kick his trash when the time came.

The duke's only mistake since escaping prison three weeks ago was getting desperate enough to access a fund that had been in his and Liz's names in Grand Cayman. Sutton had been alerted immediately, and they'd been able to retrieve the footage from the financial institution. Now, they knew exactly what the duke looked like. Creed, along with his former SEAL teammates Logan and Jace, had spent two weeks tracking Gunthry from island to island—Creed with feet on the ground and the others doing their hacking and probability analyses from Sutton's home base. It was payoff time. The duke was here. He could feel it.

Creed went to his room and hurried to shower and dress in a short-sleeved white button-down shirt and tan linen pants. He left a few buttons undone on the shirt so he would look like he fit in with the laidback vacationers. His skin was always a dark brown, and with his deep brown eyes and short facial hair, he figured he looked relaxed enough to blend in.

The Mexican restaurant he tried out was delicious. The guacamole and fish tacos rivaled the best he'd tasted. He wanted to try the carne asade too, but it had been Kiera's favorite. He wouldn't think about her, wouldn't allow himself to wonder if she still loved carne asade. Her love for him had changed, why not her taste in Mexican food?

He forced himself to eat slowly and casually, grateful the restaurant was open air so he could keep an eye out for the duke. He finished his meal and popped in the mint the waiter offered him. "Gracias." He pulled out a hundred and slipped it into the waiter's palm.

The waiter smiled at him and leaned closer. "What you need, señor?"

"How do you know I need something?" Creed elevated an eyebrow.

"Generous tips are included in your room fare and extra is discouraged. You're wanting a woman?"

Creed shook his head. A woman. He hadn't wanted a woman since Kiera. He wondered if she'd ever tried to contact him. How she'd reacted when she found out he was alive and she realized she'd thrown away their love on that Milo guy. He shook his head. That train had long since been derailed. He was focused on work now. He only felt guilty when he called home and heard the longing in his mom's voice. He would see them all soon. He was going home for Thanksgiving and Christmas. He would fit in a few football games, some time with his brothers, and of course, he'd be there for Emmett and Cambree's wedding in February after the Titans' season was over.

For some reason, he hadn't been able to bring himself to go home for the past two months, and Sutton had kept his promise of assignments that kept him away from America and any knowledge of social media and the danger of hearing Kiera Richins' name. Surprisingly, even his SEAL teammates had honored that request, not updating him on Kiera's status or rubbing in his heartbreak.

You would think he could forget, but there were too many memories of Kiera. She'd betrayed him, and the anger festered, simmering below the surface. He'd saved himself for her through pain and torture, and she'd shacked up with the first guy she had found after Creed had been pronounced dead. It hurt too much to even think about it. His mom had tried to bring up her name a few times, but he'd shut that conversation down quickly.

"A man?" the waiter asked.

Creed nodded, and the waiter looked him over. "I would not have guessed that."

"Not like that." Creed rolled his eyes. He pulled out the picture they had of the duke. "Have you seen this guy?"

The waiter studied the picture and crumpled the bill in his palm. "I've seen the idiota, yes."

"He's staying here?"

The waiter nodded.

Creed stood and clapped him on the shoulder. "Gracias."

"Be careful, señor." The waiter sort of shuddered. "Bad man. Bad connections."

Creed exhaled through his nose. "Believe me, I know that." He glanced steadily at the waiter. "What do you know?"

The waiter studied him. "I know little, but he has recruited help that is rotten."

Sutton warned him Gunthry would never be without henchmen.

Creed waited, appraising the man, wondering if he knew more. The waiter didn't flinch, and Creed finally released his gaze. "We never talked."

The waiter nodded vigorously. "I happily remember that." He bustled away.

Creed felt a chill wash over him. He knew the duke was one of the vilest men on earth. He'd abused his wife and daughter, treating them like slaves. He'd had an entire village annihilated to frame Sutton Smith and steal Liz from him when they were young. The duke had even been heavily involved in human trafficking. Creed could usually detach himself from missions, but he felt a personal connection here. Sutton and Liz had been good to him, treating him like family. Liz's daughter Ally had married River Duncan, a man Creed had looked up to his entire life. A fellow Long Islander with lots of brothers, River had joined the SEALs a couple years before Creed had, and Creed had played football with River's younger brother, Tennison. Creed had heard one too many awful stories about the duke, including how his men had beaten, drugged, and tried to drown River in the ocean in Kauai. Creed didn't want to live in a world where James Gunthry ran free. And he didn't want James Gunthry running free in a world where people he cared about lived.

He wandered along the softly-lit pathways through the multiple pool areas. He heard Latin music and immediately thought of Kiera. He cursed himself. Her memory assaulted him at the worst possible times. Though she had excelled at ballet, salsa had been one of her favorite styles of dance. Creed could easily recall the feel of her in his arms as she taught him how to dance. Then he had taught her how to kiss. His stomach heated up, and he forced the memory away, walking toward the north end of the property where the music filtered out of an open door.

This wasn't one of the areas he had seen today. It was a large theater for visiting comedians, magicians, and local entertainment as well. The front desk staff had boasted that even the Blue Man Group had performed here. When he'd toured the facility earlier, they'd been getting the theater ready for tonight's performance. Maybe the duke was inside enjoying the show. Might be one of the last things he enjoyed before returning to prison. Creed smiled as he eased in the back door. He just had to get a visual then Sutton would be en route. He couldn't wait to see Sutton slam the duke to the ground before shipping him back to an English prison.

Creed scooted along the back wall, noting that the crowd was large and very involved in the show. He didn't spot the duke on his first perusal and he focused on the stage and the performer. His smile disappeared, and his heart started racing. Creed's body chilled and exploded with heat at the same time. He couldn't move, and catching a breath was difficult. How was it possible?

Dancing on the stage, beaming for the packed theater was Kiera. She moved around the stage effortlessly, beautifully, the Latin music pulsing through the room, and Creed's pulse slammed against his throat. He felt like he was going to either choke or pass out. He wanted to sprint up there, leap onto the stage, and pull Kiera into his arms. How could she be here? Why? When he'd last seen her in Vegas, she was at the top of the performing world. She was dancing on the biggest stages with the biggest stars. He'd even heard that she was hosting a dancing show on television. And here she danced, in a silky floral dress that was too low cut on the chest and too high cut on the thigh for his blood pressure. He cast an angry glance around the room and could see the crowd was mostly men, gawking and leering at his Kiera. Yet she wasn't his Kiera, not anymore.

He searched for the blond guy she'd been with in Vegas and didn't see him, but he did finally spot another blond man. The duke. Right in the front row, lapping up Kiera's every move.

"I need a partner." Kiera called out. Men rushed at the stage, and she laughed seductively. Creed was going to thump every one of them. He started forward but froze as Kiera pointed right at the duke. No!

The duke strutted onto the stage. Creed supposed women would think Gunthry was fit and handsome if they didn't know what a snake he was. The duke wrapped his arms around Kiera's bare back, and they started dancing. Creed was going to vomit, right after he ripped the Duke's arms off. He wound his way through the crowd, hardly able to stand watching Gunthry touching Kiera. She was all smiles, and Gunthry was all sultry looks. The man deserved to die, and Creed was going to happily fulfill the job. Then he'd kiss that smile right off Kiera's beautiful face. He'd probably get arrested and thrown in a Mexican prison, but Sutton would come and get him out, thank him for killing Gunthry, and give him a new assignment so he could somehow forget Kiera. He prayed for strength for the upcoming encounter. He'd kill Gunthry bare handed so he didn't risk hurting Kiera or anyone else. He doubted his prayers were doing any good. He was pretty sure the good Lord must hate him to play such a cruel trick on him—Kiera in Gunthry's arms.

He felt his phone buzz in his pocket when he was still twenty feet from the stage. Yanking it out, he glanced at the screen. Sutton. He glanced up at Kiera and Gunthry. Sutton might not approve of him tearing the duke apart when he was only supposed to find him and then back off and wait for Sutton and the guys from MI6.

Rage filled him. Luckily, the music was loud enough to cover the growl that escaped. The couple closest to him looked at him strangely. Creed held up his phone as an excuse and stalked back the way he'd come. He would take the call outside, and maybe he'd cool off enough to listen to Sutton's advice on how to proceed. Maybe.

"Yes?" he muttered into the phone.

"Everything all right?" Sutton asked.

"I found Gunthry."

"Good." Sutton paused. "Why do you sound like somebody scalped your cat?"

"He's dancing with Kiera right now." Creed snarled, grasping the phone so tightly he wondered that it didn't crumple in his grasp.

"Kiera Richins?" Sutton's voice was surprised. Sutton was never surprised. He had more intel and knew more than anyone on planet earth, or so it seemed.

"Yes." Anger rolled through him but so did a longing for all that had been good in his life. Before he and his team had been captured. Before he'd lost Kiera. Three months of torture and imprisonment seemed to pale in comparison to this.

"I thought she was in Africa."

Creed didn't have time to demand why Kiera was in Africa. "Well, she's dancing with Gunthry right now."

"And you didn't cut in?" Sutton asked drily.

"You called, or I would've killed him." He admitted.

"I've been there," Sutton muttered.

Creed felt closer to Sutton at the moment than his own father. "Sir, what do you want me to do?"

"The humility of that statement is singularly impressive, son."

"I'm so ready to rip him apart, throw her over my shoulder, and lock her away for the rest of her life."

Sutton chuckled. "Been there too."

Creed drew in a breath and leaned against the exterior wall of the theater. The music was still thrumming inside, and he didn't want to think about what was happening. Was Gunthry still touching Kiera? Guaranteed, she was still moving her beautiful body for all to see. He used to love to see her dance, but tonight, it had ticked him off to no end.

"I don't really trust myself to make sane decisions at the moment," Creed muttered.

"I understand. Can you keep an eye on Gunthry until I can fly to London and get the MI6 guys and the proper paperwork for extraction and then fly to you?"

"Keep an eye on him alive or his corpse?"

Sutton laughed. "We actually need him alive. Can I trust you to stay in control, Creed?"

Creed paused for probably too long, but if the Navy had taught him anything, it was self-control. "Yes, sir."

"Don't underestimate him, soldier. I made that mistake once, and it almost cost me Liz."

Creed's eyes widened, surprised Sutton would be so honest with him. "I won't underestimate him."

"You think he's alone. He's not. You think he's older and could easily be subdued. You're wrong. Gunthry's a spineless prat, but he's also brilliant and devious, and I guarantee he has bodyguards and henchmen close by."

Creed blew out a breath. "So me beating him for touching Kiera might not be the best plan of action?"

"I know your fighting abilities, Creed, but if you attack Gunthry without backup, I'm betting on armed and well-trained men coming out of the shadows."

Sutton had warned him before he started the mission that Gunthry was most likely Hitler reincarnated and to be very careful. Creed had let his guard slip in the relaxed beach atmosphere, and seeing Kiera had thrown him completely off his game. His eyes darted around the shadows, but he didn't sense anyone nearby.

"Can you keep your hands off of Kiera?" Sutton asked.

"Probably not."

"I appreciate the honesty. I understand if you need to talk things out with her. Just remember, son, things aren't always as they seem."

Creed grunted in response. Talk? He wasn't going to talk to Kiera. He was going to kiss her, tell her off, and ship her home to her mama.

"You haven't been keen to hear anything about her"—Sutton's voice cut through his planning—"but I tried to tell you. She isn't with Milo anymore."

Creed didn't know how to explain that his broken heart and Kiera's broken promises transcended a mere man. "It's not about that, sir."

"Be kind, Creed."

Kind? "I would never hurt a woman, sir."

"I know that, but there are ways to hurt someone that aren't physical."

Creed nodded, though Sutton couldn't see him.

"Heart of a warrior," Sutton said.

"Heart of a warrior," Creed repeated automatically. He pushed end on his phone and let it settle in his pocket. Though he didn't know if he was strong enough, he crept around the corner and glanced in the open door. There were multiple couples on the stage now, and Kiera was walking around, instructing and smiling. The breath whooshed out of him. How he'd missed her. He would give up everything he owned and every experience he'd had simply to have all the crap between them washed away and to be able to hold her close without questions and regrets.

He folded his arms across his chest and eased into the room to stand watch. He quickly realized he needed to be incognito and forced himself to work his way into an empty chair from which he glowered at the stage. He would keep tabs on Gunthry and trail him to his room so he could bug it. Once Gunthry was secure, Creed and Kiera were going to talk.

CHAPTER SIX

After finishing her exhausting performance, all Kiera wanted to do was take a shower and order room service. She exited the stage area and headed toward her building. A hand on her arm stopped her. Whirling around, she came face to face with the blond man she'd danced with tonight.

"Hello, beautiful." He had an English accent and a smooth tongue.

Kiera gave him a forced smile. "Excuse me," she murmured. She'd told enough yahoos "not interested" to understand you had to keep it short and sweet and move away quick.

"Wait." He tightened his hold on her arm. It wasn't painful, but it was clear he wanted to be in charge. "Fancy a bit of late supper?"

Kiera shook her head. "Sorry." He looked too old for her, probably late thirties or early forties, definitely some plastic surgery. The man was handsome, and she liked his accent, but she wasn't partial to blond men. Dark hair, dark eyes, and tanned skin with short facial hair. There she went picturing Creed, as usual. He'd made it more than obvious he didn't want her when he'd returned from the dead. Months had passed, and the cretin still hadn't so much as called her. She knew Creed could track a shark through the ocean. If he wanted to, he would've found her on her travels through Thailand, the Philippines, Africa, and now the Caribbean.

The beautiful, innocent children on her service trips had helped her push her pain to the back of her mind. Yet her heart would never heal. If only she could tell her heart to forget about Creed. Sadly, hearts didn't work like that.

"Maybe tomorrow?" The man persisted.

"Maybe." She nodded to him and walked past. She didn't think he followed, but as she walked along the dimly-lit pathways back to her suite, she could sense someone was following her. She thought about calling security, but for some reason, she wasn't afraid. She could simply sense a presence.

Maybe someone from the show was enamored with her. She'd been a big name once. Now, she was a washed-up has been. Lately, she'd focused on charity performances, and though she hadn't been able to forget Creed, she'd thoroughly enjoyed seeing new lands and meeting the people, especially the children. She'd also worked at several gorgeous resorts like this. The pay was fine at the resorts, nothing close to what she'd made when she'd starred in Vegas, L.A., London, and New York, but she didn't really care much about the pay. She was happy to be far from America and the painful memories of Creed.

She took the elevator to her twelfth-floor penthouse suite. The resort treated her like she was still something special and had told her she could stay as long as she wanted. She only had to do the performance every few nights. They had a lot of other entertainment coming in.

Finally entering her room, she slid out of her heels, slipped her dress over her head and took a long shower before sliding into a floral, silk robe and blow drying her hair quickly and tying it back in a ponytail. She grabbed the room service menu. Supposedly, the Japanese restaurant was to die for. She could really go for a dragon roll and a crazy boy with no siracha right now. Ooh, and a shrimp tempura appetizer. She dialed room service and placed an order for way too much food, knowing she would never eat it all. She'd lost too much weight when Creed died and still struggled to eat a full meal.

Kiera stretched out on the king-sized bed in the master bedroom and sighed. It was comfy. Maybe she would take a short nap before dinner. Then she would stay up reading or watching a movie or something. What did she have to do tomorrow besides exercise and lay on the beach, being gracious to tourists who recognized her? She used to practice twelve to fourteen hours a day, but maintaining her fitness level was enough for the type of dancing she was doing currently.

There was a sharp rap at the door. That was quick. Kiera pushed off the bed and tightened the robe. She hurried to the door and opened it a crack. Glancing out, she expected to see dinner containers and a smiling attendant. Instead, she saw a glowering man with dark hair, dark eyes, tanned skin, and the perfect length of facial hair.

"Creed?" The world started spinning around her, and then everything went black.

She crumpled to the floor but could hear a voice floating above her. A voice she'd dreamed of hearing so often she knew it couldn't be reality. The voice came from far above, just like Creed was far away and would never be here for her again.

"Kiera? Kiera?" Creed's voice finally registered. It had to be him. She knew that voice like she knew her dance routines.

Kiera shook her head. She'd really lost it now. She'd dreamed Creed was at her door, and now, she was hearing his voice.

The door pushed softly against her, and she stirred, scrambling away from it.

"Kiera?" Creed truly stood above her in the doorway.

No. Creed coming for her was a dream she'd burned months ago, okay maybe weeks, but she had finally burned it and locked her heart away from the pain. Hadn't she?

He pushed the door open a little farther and slipped inside. The door closed behind him, and Kiera couldn't budge from off the floor. She stared up at his perfect face. She'd forgotten how huge he was—almost six four. He had so much muscle it made her mouth go dry. The white shirt showed off his tanned skin, and a few undone buttons revealed his muscular chest.

She shook her head. She must be in shock. Creed couldn't be here. Creed had ditched her and didn't love her. Why would he follow her to Cancun? He had much more important jobs to do other than tracking her down.

Creed bent down, wrapped his hands around her waist and easily plucked her to her feet. She'd been lifted so many times in her career, sometimes even pretending to be vulnerable or wounded for her part, but she'd assisted her partner with every lift. Creed had just lifted her as a dead weight. He was impossibly strong, and she was like a limp noodle. She leaned heavily against him.

"Kiera." His voice went all soft and husky, and the way he

was studying her made her feel warm and prickly from head to toe. Oh, how she'd loved him.

He wrapped his arms around her back and gently pulled her close. Kiera had no clue how to respond to this very real-feeling hallucination. "C-creed," she whispered, not returning his hug, but loving the feel of his muscled chest pressing against her.

"Now come on, love. You can do better than that."

"What?" She was so confused. She stared up into his dark eyes, and they were twinkling at her like they always used to do. All the angst, pain, and confusion of losing him disappeared and there was just her and Creed. No matter what had come between them before they were together now. It was so simple and beautiful.

"This is *not* a hug. A hug involves two bodies, four arms, and lots and lots of contact." He winked. "Shall we give it another go?"

Tears sprang from her eyes as she stared at his handsome face and charming smile. She threw her arms around his neck and clung to him. Creed had said a similar line to her the very first time he hugged her. She'd been young and had never even held hands with a boy. She'd felt extremely awkward when the cutest boy at school had given her attention then hugged her at a party after a home football game.

"Ah, that's better." Creed groaned, and the warmth and desire in that groan filled her stomach with heat.

Kiera thought it was more than better. It was absolute perfection. Her head fit in the crook of his neck like they were built to come together. *Creed!* Her heart seemed to be cheering. Creed was truly here and holding her like she'd dreamed of so many times. It had taken him too long to find her, but he'd finally come for her and that was all that mattered.

He ran his hands along her back, and it felt like heaven with the silk sliding against her skin and Creed's warm hands doing a number on her nervous system. He brought one hand up and loosened her ponytail then trailed his fingers through her hair. "Kiera."

Kiera stared up at him as he bowed his head closer to hers. His mint-tinged breath and his warm, sensuous cologne made her stomach flutter. It was the cologne she'd bought him for Christmas one year—Burberry. It had a great mix of cinnamon, amber, and tarragon and made her want to melt every time she smelled it on him.

Creed was here. He was alive, and he was holding her. His breath brushed her lips, and Kiera sighed with longing. How she'd missed him, missed his touch. She arched up to kiss him as he whispered, "Oh man, I'm going to regret this in the morning."

Then he was kissing her, and her brain couldn't process anything but the pressure of his lips on hers. They'd been made to kiss each other. There was nothing on Earth she loved more than dancing except this. Creed always had a rhythm to his kisses, a natural and instinctive choreography, and tonight was the perfect arrangement for her. He started hard and fast, capturing her lips and conveying how he'd hungered for her. How they'd been apart for far too long. She returned the hunger and then some. This kiss was the kiss of a warrior who had won the battle and was back to claim what was due to him. Kiera should've protested that she wasn't the girl waiting for the hunky hero anymore, but there was no strength in her to protest, only to savor and fully return his mind-blowing kiss.

After several blissful, heat-filled minutes, he slowed the kisses down and took his time exploring her lips and mouth. It was like he was tasting her and savoring her and couldn't get enough. Kiera's body hummed with awareness and desire from her mouth out. She could never get enough of him. Finally, the pain of separation, the waiting to be together was over. She was right where she was meant to be—in Creed's arms and being swept away by his kisses.

Kiera's head was so cloudy and full of Creed that she couldn't stand on her own two feet. Luckily, she didn't need to with his strong arms holding her close, burning fire through her thin robe. She held on tight to his broad back and let him work his magic on her mouth.

His lips left hers and slowly trailed down her neck, leaving fire in their wake. He was working his way back up to her lips, and she could hardly stand the wait, but then he broke away and straightened, muttering, "I can't do this."

Kiera blinked at him, confused and wanting him to keep kissing her. He couldn't do ... what exactly? He stepped back, released his hold on her and shoved a hand through his hair, staring broodily down at her.

He said nothing, and Kiera was chilled and shaky, swaying on her feet. She'd been ripped too quickly from his heat and touch. It was like being in a steam room then jumping into an ice-cold pool. Her head cleared bit by bit, and she thought of what he'd said right before he kissed her. "Why are you going to regret kissing me in the morning?"

Creed blew out a breath, and now instead of broody, he was openly glaring at her. "You need to put some clothes on."

Kiera reared back and glanced down at her robe. It covered her, going clear down to her knees with double sashes at her waist that were both tied tight. Most of her stage costumes were more revealing. She folded her arms across her chest and glared at him. "No. Right now, you need to explain ... lots of things."

Creed glanced at her robe before meeting her gaze. "*I* need to explain?" He put a hand to his chest. "That's exactly what I was thinking. *I'm* the one who needs to explain."

The sarcasm dripped from his voice, but she wasn't about to back down. "Exactly," she said, not giving an inch. "You can start with why you 'can't do this,' said right after we kissed. Then explain 'I'm going to regret this in the morning' being said right before we kissed. Then we can go back to hmm, I don't know, you being not dead and never coming for me, and making me wish you *were* dead!" She pushed out a frustrated breath, clenching her fists when she wanted to pound on his chest. Yet she didn't trust herself to touch him right now. Too much risk of getting lost in him again and losing her well-deserved anger.

"Why are you even here?" she shot at him.

Creed gave her a dry chuckle. "I'm not here to talk to you Kiera, and I'm definitely not here to kiss you. I'm here to give you a warning."

Kiera's heart had already shriveled and died when he was confirmed dead, but when he came back to life and never came for her, her heart turned into a rock. Somehow, miraculously it could still hurt though. This wasn't him coming for her. Of course, it wasn't. He regretted even kissing her. Why was she even surprised?

"I'm a big girl. I can take care of myself without Mr. Bad-A Navy SEAL taking pity on my sorry self and coming to watch out for me."

Creed took a step closer to her. Kiera stood her ground. The man who used to love and adore her was now trying to intimidate her. Why had she loved this cretin so desperately? She glanced over his beautifully-sculpted face and body. Besides his irresistible looks, he used to be fun, smart, charming, and nice. Now, he was simply the man who had never cared about her enough to return to her. The man who had killed her heart.

"Stay away from the older blond guy. The one with the lame English accent."

It was easy to know who he meant. There'd only been a few blond men at the show tonight, only one she'd danced with, and only one who had an accent.

"Didn't seem much older to me, pretty hot and fit actually."

Creed's jaw clamped tight, and a muscle worked in it. Kiera wanted to reach up and touch his jaw. Tell him she'd do what he asked if only he'd hold her again. She clamped her arms tighter around herself.

"Don't you dare, Kiera. You just try and date him, and you'll see what kind of a bad-A Navy SEAL I am."

If she wasn't so ticked at him, he would be inspiring to behold right now. All that muscle and raw determination. She could feel the strength radiating from him. She'd never been afraid of Creed, never would be, but she could imagine if someone was on his wrong side they'd be in peril.

Yet he had no desire to be with her, and the blond guy seemed to tick him off. Hmm. She wasn't above using that to tick him off more. Turnabout was fair play. She'd been broken since he rejected her without having the guts to actually do it face to face. Simply sending her some Dear Jane letter that she'd wrongly assumed meant he loved her and wanted her happiness above all else. Now, she realized it was just a cop-out. *Go live your life, go be happy*. Then the dream-ruiner had been brought back to life and run away on his "missions." He'd left her with nothing, her and her stone of a heart.

A rap came at the door, and Creed glowered at her. “Expecting someone?”

“Actually, I was.” She raised an eyebrow and watched the emotions race across his face—anger and jealousy warring with one another. Maybe there was something left in him that cared about her.

She pushed around him to get the door. Creed caught her arm and pulled her back against his chest. The breath rushed out of her. She molded to his body perfectly. His arms came around her waist, and Kiera couldn’t help but sigh with longing for him. The thin robe wasn’t nearly enough to protect her from the heat and possessiveness of his arms. The exquisite strength of his chest muscles pressing against her back.

He bent close and whispered in her ear, “Who’s at the door, Kiera?”

Kiera tilted her head to meet his dark gaze and gave him a look full of challenge. Let him think she’d invited a room full of men over for all she cared. “Something I’ve been craving all day,” she whispered.

His eyes darkened to almost black, and his arms tightened around her. If she wasn’t so ticked off, she would’ve loved every second of being this close to Creed. The protectiveness and desire in his embrace were so familiar yet thrilling. She’d been without him, craved him, for too long, and she was in danger of falling for him all over again.

“You’d better ask him to leave unless you want to watch me decimate the man on your doorstep,” he threatened in a low growl.

“I don’t think you even understand who you’re competing with.” She gave him a condescending glare.

“No one stands a chance against me.”

Kiera thought that was probably true. The knock came again.

"Who is it Kiera?" Creed's eyes were narrowed and full of protective intent. Kiera wanted to tell him that he had no right to be protective of her anymore, but she worried about pushing him too far, afraid for the poor room service attendant on the other side of the door.

She looked into Creed's gaze and whispered back, "Room service."

Creed stared in disbelief. Then he started laughing. She loved the rumble of laughter in his chest pressing against her back. Kiera couldn't help but laugh along with him.

"I thought ..." He shook his head and released her.

Kiera's laughter died quickly. She wasn't sure she wanted to know what he'd thought, and she hated that him touching her again was a craving she would never be able to satiate.

She went and opened the door. A smiling young man rolled the serving dolly in and unloaded several trays onto the table.

"Gracias," Kiera said.

Creed palmed him a twenty, and the young man walked out the door grinning.

"You're not supposed to tip them. They were very specific about that when I checked in."

"None of them have complained yet," Creed said.

"You don't need to act like a billionaire."

He didn't even respond. He stared over the various plates of food with a furrowed brow. The anger was back in his eyes, and she wasn't sure why. Hadn't they just laughed together? It didn't change anything, couldn't fix the pain of him not wanting her, but couldn't they somehow, someway talk this out? No. Nothing he could say would make up for the way he'd deserted her. Him dying had been horrific, but she'd never blamed him. Him being brought back to life but not coming for her? That she blamed him for aplenty. Yet what if he'd been tortured so horribly it had ruined his mind and his ability to love? Maybe that was why he didn't want her anymore. Being around him right now, he seemed like the old Creed. Her Creed. No. She couldn't think like that ever again.

Creed uncovered platters, and a ghost of a smile touched his lips. "You and your sushi." Then the smile was gone. "Who are you expecting, Kiera?"

She stared at him. "What?"

Creed strode away from the table and got right in her space. Kiera did back away this time. Creed kept coming until she was backed into a wall.

"The Kiera I knew would never order this much food, knowing she could only eat a fraction of it. The Kiera I knew hated to waste. She was too worried about those who didn't have enough food. Taught well by her philanthropist mama."

He didn't know her anymore, and even though her breath was coming in fast pants from his nearness, he was ticking her off. She wished her body didn't respond to him so readily, like muscle memory. It reminded her of dancing the merengue, so easy a drunk person could do it and so natural as soon as the music started playing you couldn't help but dance along. Creed came near, and her body immediately flooded with heat and wanted to touch him and move in rhythm with him.

"You don't know me anymore," she whispered, getting caught up in his dark, stormy gaze.

Creed swallowed, and his body brushed against hers. "That's for sure." He stepped back and glowered at her. "I'm only going to ask one more time. Who were you expecting ... wearing that?" His eyes traveled over her robe.

"I'm only going to ask once. Get out." She pointed at the door. Unfortunately, her hand was shaking. Why was Creed acting like she was some loose woman? They'd made a pact in high school to never let the fire of their love get out of control, to save themselves for marriage. He'd tried a few times to push farther than they should, and she'd helped him stay in control. The night before he left, it was her that had tried to get him to break the pact, and he'd stayed strong. Their love was stronger than a mere physical bond. That's what he always said when they were tempted. Creed had to know she wouldn't be waiting for someone in her suite in nothing but a robe.

Creed blinked at her and bent down close again. "I thought what we used to have was special to you, but obviously, you aren't the Kiera I fell in love with."

Kiera slapped him across the face. The slap rang through the room, and neither of them moved. Creed finally gave her his sarcastic smile. The one he gave to people he hated. "This isn't over, Kiera. I'll be watching you, and I'll protect you. Even if you don't care about protecting yourself any longer."

Kiera's stomach felt sick, and she knew all this food was going to go to waste. Her mama would be disappointed in her right now for more reasons than that. "Do I need to slap you again? Or are you leaving?"

Creed stormed to the door and threw it open. He turned and threw verbal daggers back at her. "I despise what you've become, Kiera, but if you ever cared for me at all, stay away from the blond guy."

Kiera hurried to the door and pushed at him. He didn't budge an inch. "Get out!" she screamed.

Creed smiled at her. "I'll get out, but if any other man tries to come through this door, I'll tear him apart. Sleep tight." He waved and stepped out onto the wide patio.

Kiera slammed the door shut and screamed a gargled, "Argh! I hate you Creed Hawk!"

She could hear his laughter on the other side of the door. Running to the bedroom, she threw herself down on the bed. Anger still rushed through her, but the sadness wasn't far behind. Creed was here. He hadn't come for her. He didn't care about her. And now, for some reason, he thought she was a floozy. There had been those rumors of her and Milo living together, but Creed wouldn't believe that kind of smut. At least, her Creed wouldn't. He'd really said that he despised what she'd become. What kind of rotten thing was that to say? Why had he kissed her like that? Just to torture her and make her see all she was missing not being in his arms? Tears wet the pillow beneath her face. She had loved him for so long and so deeply, he'd been her inspiration and her every dream. Now everything they'd once shared was tainted and ugly.

She brushed the tears off and made a promise to herself. Next time the blond English guy asked her to dinner, she was going. She could only pray Creed would go insane with jealousy. He obviously didn't love her anymore, and she had no clue why he was treating her so horribly, but she could see the jealousy on his face, and he'd kissed her like he still wanted her. Even if all she had was the ability to make him hurt like he'd hurt her. She would take it.

CHAPTER SEVEN

Kiera woke early to go lift weights at the gym. Even though her career had taken a nosedive in the past two months since Creed had returned from the dead and she'd given up on life instead of fighting for herself and her reputation, she still loved to move and exercise. Maybe someday she would get back to television or Broadway, but neither appealed to her anymore. Right now, she was taking one day at a time. One day at a time might be asking too much of herself with Creed appearing last night. Why was he here? He'd explained nothing last night besides warning her away from the guy with the English accent, kissing the dickens out her, and breaking her heart all over again. When a stone heart shattered, could it ever be repaired? She doubted it.

She was doing a bent-over row in the free weight area when she sensed his presence. Straightening too quickly, she felt a little lightheaded and had to hold on to the weight rack for a second. She searched the large gym area and saw him. Creed was using the cable machine and wearing a blue tank top and gray shorts. The muscles in his back and arms rippled as he pulled the cables into his chest. Kiera sucked in a breath, feeling more lightheaded than she had when she'd stood too quickly.

She forced herself to face forward, grab lighter weights, and do a bicep curl. Her eyes kept straying to Creed though, and it was a struggle to keep good form. His gaze met hers a few times in the mirror, and he gave her his trademark grin. Her stomach would swoop predictably, and her face would get all flushed and hot. She cussed herself. She used to be a professional, world-renowned dancer. Her life was about self-control and discipline. Why couldn't she find an ounce of self-control anytime that man came within a hundred yards of her?

She re-shelved the fifteen-pound dumbbells and walked to the juice and water station. Maybe something cool would quench the fire for Creed that she couldn't seem to tamp down. Glancing in his direction, she saw he was moving her way quickly. She turned to avoid him, but he was too fast. He brushed against her and wrapped his arms around her elbows as if to steady her. Her eyes narrowed. He'd done that on purpose. He had no right to touch her anymore.

"Excuse me," he murmured, a slight smile decorating his handsome face. "I couldn't help but notice you."

"You noticed little old me?" She put a hand to her heart and gave him a fake Southern drawl. She wanted to yell and scream, but fake sugar, like the nasty aftertaste of saccharin on her tongue, would be almost as effective. Especially in a public setting.

He leaned closer and murmured, "Always."

Kiera's heart raced, but she folded her arms across her chest and scooted away from his touch and smell. What game was he playing this morning? Acting like he didn't know her then making her want to throw herself against that beautifully-formed chest of his. She wasn't falling into his trap. She was done with Creed Hawk. "You seem to know your way around a weight room." She fluttered her eyelashes and then let her gaze travel over him slowly. It was torture checking him out, knowing he'd never be hers again, knowing her head would never fit in the perfect crook of his neck while his strong arms surrounded her. It was worse than being denied chocolate for life and living in Hershey, Pennsylvania.

"Would you like some help lifting?" he asked.

"Oh!" She placed a hand over her mouth. "What a sweetie. Are you a personal trainer or something?"

He chuckled. "Or something."

"I'd love some help from a big, buff stud like you." She ran her tongue over her lips, wondering if she was putting it on too strong, but Creed deserved every second of crap she could dish out. He was the one who'd killed her heart, and now, he was pretending he didn't know her. She knew he'd easily read through her sugar answers to the deep-seated sarcasm. She didn't need help from anyone, and she especially didn't need help from him. She thought of a way to tick him off even worse. "Wait a minute. I know you!"

His face froze. "Do you now?"

"You're one of those famous Hawk brothers. You all are so handsome and look just alike."

Creed smiled, but it wasn't his genuine smile. It was all military and tight self-control.

"Now which one are you?" She tapped her finger on her lips. "The studly football player?"

"No. That's Emmett."

"Oh? Yes, Emmett's amazing. I love watching his beautiful

biceps when he stretches out to catch a football." She smiled, hoping she was ticking him off. "So, if not the football player, then you have to be ... the world-acclaimed extreme athlete. The one who surfs waves no one dares surf and jumps out of planes without a chute."

Creed rolled his eyes. "Bridger."

"Yes, Bridger. He's so brave." She bit at her lip and almost laughed at his rigid face. "Not Bridger. I can't remember the other ones ... Oh! Yes, I do. You're the multi-billionaire who is simply brilliant and keeps getting the Most Eligible Bachelor of the Year Award. Owns half the country or something."

Creed laughed, but she could tell he wasn't amused. "That's Callum."

"Huh. I really like Callum." It was a lie. Callum was a good guy but the least friendly of the crew. "So what do *you* do?" She made her eyes all big and interested. Truthfully, she thought Creed's profession was the noblest and the bravest, but at the same time, it had robbed her of the man she loved. He deserved to think she didn't care about him one whit for making her want him so horribly last night and then ditching her all over again.

"I'm in private security."

"Isn't that ... exciting?" She gave him a fake smile and used body language to show a sharp drop in her interest in him. She'd practiced the drop of her shoulder and twist of her knee a hundred times for a routine in the semi-finals of *Just Dance*. "Hmm. Must be tough being surrounded by all those famous brothers." One thing that had always impressed her about Creed was, even though he was fiercely competitive, he always supported and cheered for his brothers. He'd known his path would be military, and he'd taken it and excelled, but she wasn't about to admit how impressive he was to her.

"It has its moments."

"I bet." She elevated her eyebrows and completed the lost interest motion—head dipped away, spin on her far heel. "You know, I think I'll just lift on my own today, but thanks so much for the offer."

"That's too bad." Creed's gaze traveled over her slowly. "I guess you lost your chance."

Kiera's body chilled, and it was all she could to not slap him like she'd done last night. She turned and rushed away without looking back at him. She'd definitely lost her chance—for happiness with Creed, for success in life. Truly, she'd lost everything when he deserted her. And she knew she'd never get Creed back, which made everything else in her life lose its luster.

CHAPTER EIGHT

Creed made it through his workout, but his eyes kept straying to Kiera. He hadn't been able to resist studying her and had finally let himself approach her. It had been almost like old times to pretend he didn't know her and flirt, even though he knew the sugar-sweet responses were verbal daggers. Those daggers turned to bullets when she listed his brothers' accomplishments. He was proud of his brothers and their paths, and even though they competed and wrestled, he always cheered louder than anyone else for each of their successes. Yet he wanted Kiera to think he was the best of all of them. *His* Kiera had always been super proud of his calling in life, his desire to protect and serve. He wasn't sure he even knew this Kiera who was making him second guess everything he'd known about her and even though he was confused and hurt he wanted to just throw her over his shoulder and paddle her rear and then maybe run for a preacher or a Vegas wedding chapel. Knowing she'd been with another man, probably multiple men, helped him cool his desires and keep his dreams of being with her at bay.

When she left the gym, he followed, making sure she got back to her room safely. An hour later, she headed out again, wearing a white lace cover-up over a pink swimsuit. He swallowed down his desire for her and waited a few minutes to make sure she didn't return to her room, then broke in and installed a miniscule security camera and sensors focused on the main area and the exterior door. He'd be alerted whenever she opened the door and would be able to watch what was going on. He'd found out the duke's room number last night and had been able to install similar devices this morning while the loser was showering. Checking his watch screen, he confirmed the duke was still eating his breakfast at his suite table.

Creed headed down to the pool areas, hoping Kiera would be staying at the resort rather than going on a day trip. It would help his blood pressure a lot. This area was a hotbed for traffickers and crime against Americans, and no matter that he and Kiera weren't together anymore, he could not handle the thought of anything happening to her. That gave him an unfamiliar rush of guilt. Kiera had suffered through him supposedly dying. He'd tried when he was imprisoned not to think too much about how his family or Kiera was dealing with it. A man could go insane stewing over something like that. Maybe that was why Kiera had given herself to another man. Maybe it had been too much for her. He shook his head. She'd moved on quickly enough. She obviously didn't feel the level of love he'd felt for her.

He sauntered through the pool areas but didn't see her anywhere. An alert on his phone sounded. He paused and glanced at it. The duke was leaving his room, dressed in a floral swimsuit. He didn't look like he had anything but his swimsuit and flip flops. Good. The duke would stay close by, which would make Creed's day easier. Just as long as Gunthry stayed away from Kiera.

Creed approached the last section of pools. They were infinity pools and hot tubs that overlooked the beach and ocean beyond. Kiera was floating on her back in the pool to the south. Creed sucked in a breath. Her dark hair streamed out away from her beautiful face. Her eyes were closed, and she looked so peaceful and innocent. Like the Kiera he'd planned his life around. Her deep brown skin was smooth and firm, and the pale pink suit showed off her shape to perfection.

Her eyes fluttered open. Then she stood in the chest deep water. She glanced around, and her gaze landed on him. Creed didn't try to act like he hadn't been gawking at her. He tilted his chin up. He should've smiled or waved, done something more friendly, but he was too lost in her gaze.

She stared at him for a few seconds and then dove under the water and swam away from him. She was like a beautiful siren, and he would follow her anywhere. Walking around the huge pool, he kept her in his sights. She pulled herself out of the water, and droplets glistened on her gorgeous skin.

Creed was twenty feet away, not sure that being lured in by her was smart, but how could he resist? Kiera glanced his way and gave him a sweet smile. Creed's heartbeat increased. Maybe she wanted to be with him. He tried to hold on to his righteous anger over how she'd betrayed him, but it was getting harder and harder. Maybe if he spent the day with her, they could talk it all out, move past the hurt. He returned the smile and increased his pace.

A blond man in a floral swimsuit walked up to Kiera with a

drink in hand. Creed cursed and turned away. The duke didn't know who Creed was, but it was smarter not to get on the man's radar if he did notice Creed keeping an eye on him at some point. His SEAL buddies claimed he was so stealthy he could track an owl and never be heard, but Sutton had told him several times not to underestimate the duke.

Creed walked behind a set of pillars and inched his way closer.

"A piña colada for the beautiful lady," Gunthry said.

"Oh, no thank you."

"What are your plans today?"

"I'm hoping to relax in the sun and listen to the ocean," Kiera said.

Creed hoped that wasn't an invitation. Of course, Gunthry took it as one, the creep. "Sounds perfect. I'll join you."

Creed crept out of his hiding spot and watched Kiera and Gunthry walk down the steps to the beach and settle side by side in a large cabana bed. His blood boiled. What was she thinking? He'd warned her to stay away from the duke, but she definitely wasn't listening to his advice. All the anger from last night when he'd had to watch them dance resurfaced. Would Sutton think he was justified in pummeling the duke and jeopardizing the mission when the man hadn't actually done anything besides lay on a covered mattress on the beach and smile and flirt with Creed's girl? Doubtful.

Creed shoved a hand through his hair and pushed out a breath. He really couldn't do this much longer. Thank heavens Sutton would be here soon. He was surprised he hadn't received a knock on his door in the middle of the night. Sutton had his own jets, more than one, and he wanted the duke taken down badly.

His watch rang. He'd left his phone in the room. He pushed a button to answer and backed away into a shaded alcove so no one could overhear the conversation.

"Are you here?" Creed demanded of Sutton.

"It'll be at least a day, maybe two. Everything all right?"

"What?" Creed exploded. He couldn't sit around and watch Kiera flirt with Gunthry for another minute, let alone another day or two. What would he do if Gunthry kissed her. Argh! He couldn't even let himself think it.

"Corbin's got a situation and needs all of us right now. Is Gunthry a flight risk?"

"I highly doubt it." Creed scowled as Gunthry ran his fingers up Kiera's arm and she smiled sweetly at him. Flight risk. Gunthry appeared to be going nowhere but to Kiera's suite. Creed's fists clenched.

"Okay. Keep an eye on him. I'm going to send River and a few of my security team to England in my Airbus to pick up the MI6 guys and come apprehend Gunthry. They'll try to hurry, but plan on it taking River at least until tomorrow night to get there with travel time and getting all the necessary clearance to apprehend Gunthry in Mexico. Hopefully, I'll be able to fly straight there as soon as I take care of this situation with Corbin."

Creed cursed under his breath. So best case, he was spending the next day and a half watching Kiera flirt with the duke? He'd explode. "Is that our best course of action?"

"Meaning?"

"Why don't I just put a bullet between the duke's eyes right now, and we'll be done with him?"

Sutton chuckled. "Believe me, I love that idea and wish I could be the one placing that bullet, but his escape is too well-known. I'm not willing to risk my operation being shut down by Interpol for the sake of taking revenge on Gunthry."

Sutton was incredibly impressive to Creed. If Kiera had been through what Liz and Ally had with the duke, Creed would've killed him long ago.

"We go through the proper authorities, and Gunthry rots in prison. I'm sure they'll watch him and their guards more closely the next time they do a prison transfer."

Creed could only grunt in response. He hated this Gunthry guy, and he hardly knew him.

"But I wouldn't complain if a stray bullet landed between his eyes in the skirmish," Sutton said.

Creed laughed, thankful Sutton was human.

"If I didn't have so much faith in you, we'd run this differently. But it's worth putting all the pressure I can on Corbin's case until it's settled. Keep an eye on him, and we'll be there soon."

"All right sir." How else could he respond? He appreciated Sutton's faith in him, but how was he going to do nothing do but wait and watch the love of his life flirt with a murderer? Creed was too far away to hear them, but he could see them clearly. Gunthry had rolled onto his stomach, and Kiera was rubbing sunscreen into his back. No, no, no. Creed could not hack this.

"Is Kiera all right?" Sutton asked, and Creed wondered if the man truly was more than human. He had psychic powers.

"Depends on your version of all right," Creed grunted out.

"What does that mean?"

"Well currently she's rubbing sunscreen into Gunthry's back. So maybe she thinks she's all right but she's not going to be when I get my hands on her."

Sutton's silence was stony. "You need to warn her to stay away from him."

"I did." Creed forced the words out from a clamped jaw.

"Warn her again."

"I think my warnings have pushed her the other way. She's not exactly my biggest fan right now." Which ticked him off almost as much as her touching Gunthry. Creed wasn't the one who had betrayed their love. Why was she acting like him leaving to work for Sutton rather than sit around and watch her with another man was the bigger transgression?

"Blimey, Creed. You know how sadistic he is. Get her away from him."

"Even if it compromises the mission?"

Creed could feel Sutton's angst over the phone. "An innocent woman's safety is more important than the mission."

Sadly, Kiera wasn't as innocent as she used to be, but Creed appreciated more than he could explain that Sutton cared about Kiera's safety over recapturing the man who had ruined so many years of his life and tortured the woman he loved.

"Keep an eye on both of them, keep an eye out for Gunthry's men, and above all else protect Kiera. If you have to choose, choose to keep her safe."

"Thank you, sir." Even though Creed wanted to have some serious words with Kiera right now, and the sight of her touching Gunthry made him physically ill, he knew he'd protect her. "Heart of a warrior."

"Heart of a warrior."

Kiera cast one more glance back at Creed, catching his dark

gaze. He was obviously frustrated with her being with William, but William was a lot safer than Creed for her at the moment. She laid down on the beach bed underneath the cabana and closed her eyes, trying to ignore William and not think about Creed. William was the blond English guy that Creed had warned her about. He'd strutted up to her as she almost made the mistake of walking right into Creed's beautiful arms. William had saved her from letting down her guard with Creed, but then the man had acted like she'd invited him along to the beach, telling her his name and all about his successful investment business. He'd asked her to rub sunscreen on his back, which she'd tried to do quickly. He had an odd vibe and was too old for her, despite the obvious plastic surgery that made him look thirty.

William ran his fingers along her forearm. "I haven't been able to stop thinking about the mesmerizing way you dance. Would you accompany me tonight to go dancing?"

Dancing was definitely her language, but she wasn't going anywhere with this noob. "I'll have to see what the resort needs me to do tonight."

"I checked with the manager. He assured me you're free for the next three nights." He smiled silkily at her.

Kiera arched an eyebrow, not appreciating him checking her schedule. "You could've asked me."

"I just did."

Kiera forced a smile. "Excuse me. I need to use the ladies' room."

He stood as she did, and she appreciated his manners, but she didn't like the look in his too green eyes. "I'll see you soon?"

She nodded, uneasy and not sure why. She had a lot of men hitting on her, especially since her fame with *Just Dance* and all her performances since then, but she wasn't getting great feelings from this guy.

Sliding a white lace cover-up over her pink one-piece and picking up her flip-flops, she sauntered along the beach, squishing the soft sand between her toes. Walking up the first set of stairs, she dropped her flip-flops on the concrete and slipped into them before entering the nearest women's restroom. It was an excuse to get away from William, not that he could see her this far away.

She glanced around but couldn't see Creed anywhere. She wondered where he was then cursed herself for caring and for remembering how fabulous he'd looked in only swim trunks. Nothing had changed since he'd ditched her two months ago. He was obviously here for some job, and all he did was infuriate her, mostly because of her body's response to him. Well, her body could forget about it. Those bridges had collapsed under the weight of his lack of love for her.

She used the restroom and was washing her hands when the door slid open. She glanced in the mirror at the very large man walking into a women's restroom. The bright sunshine made it hard to discern the person's face. Whirling around, her heart rate doubled, until Creed's irresistible face came into view. Then it quadrupled.

"Kiera," he said all warm and loving, as if they were them again. His eyes darkened to a smolder that made it hard to resist throwing herself at him.

Kiera pulled in a breath, shaky and off-balance with him looking at her like that. "What are you doing in the women's bathroom?"

Creed crossed the short distance until he was right in front of her, inches from her actually. She couldn't resist looking over the lovely muscles of his chest as he was in nothing but teal blue swim trunks.

"You like it." He arched an eyebrow and flexed a bicep, all cocky and flirtatious.

"*What* are you doing?" she asked again, to avoid responding and revealing exactly how much she liked to look at him.

His brow furrowed, and his cocky grin disappeared. He leaned even closer, and Kiera could smell his sensual cologne and feel his warm breath on her forehead. She glanced up so she didn't keep focusing on his chest, but that was a mistake. His face was more appealing than his body, and she had nowhere to go, backed up against the bathroom counter.

"You've got to listen to me and stay away from the d—the blond guy."

Kiera pushed out a huffy breath and folded her arms across her chest to try to create some distance from him. That was another mistake as her arms brushed the taut muscles and firm skin of his chest, and heat flushed her face.

"What do you care?"

"Believe me, I care."

Kiera tried not to internalize that, but she wanted him to care far too much.

"If you cared, why did you leave last night?" She couldn't go into their past. Why he'd left her, and why, when he could've returned to her, he didn't care enough to find her.

Creed's eyes swept over her face. He let out a low growl of frustration. Then he wrapped his hands around her waist, picked her clean off her feet, and set her on the bathroom counter. Kiera gasped and wrapped her arms around his shoulders for stability. Creed pressed in closer to her, his gaze dropping to her lips before recapturing hers. He was going to kiss her, and she wanted him to, but how would her heart take it when he discarded her again?

Kiera's fingers kneaded the muscles of his shoulders with her fingertips, reveling in the firm skin and muscle. She whispered, "You're even tougher than I remembered."

Creed smiled then. "I've always been tough."

Kiera laughed at him. It was so Creed. He was overly confident and completely consumed with her, but was he truly consumed with her anymore? The look in his dark eyes said yes. Kiera couldn't resist trailing her fingers from his shoulders to his chest. She loved the feel of his smooth skin and well-developed muscles under her fingertips.

Creed let out a low groan and then muttered, "Why can I never resist you?"

Kiera gasped, frustration and irritation tracing through her. She pushed at his chest as he lowered his head to capture her mouth with his. Heat exploded through her—desire and anger combined.

The door to the bathroom swung open. Creed pulled back and turned to the elderly lady who toddled in.

"Oh? Excuse me." She giggled. "Didn't know this was the place for a kissing session."

Creed chuckled, but Kiera could hear the unsteadiness of it. She affected him. That knowledge made her soften toward him, but not enough to allow her heart to get tangled up with his and then be broken again.

Kiera slid off the counter but was still in the circle of his arms. "Excuse us," she said to the lady, pushing out of his grasp and hurrying from the bathroom.

Creed followed, grabbing her arm before she could leave the sheltered alcove of the bathrooms. His eyes shot around the pool area then focused back on her. "Stay away from that guy, Kiera."

"Or what?"

Creed's eyes narrowed. "Or I'll kiss you on the face until you don't know which way is up."

Heat flared in her abdomen, but she was angry enough to hold the attraction at bay. Right before their first kiss, they'd been placing bets on if his little brother Bridger could execute a certain skateboarding trick. The kid was the most gifted non-traditional athlete Kiera had ever seen. Creed's bet had been if Bridger could jump off their pool house roof, do a backflip, and then slide down the pool railing on his board, she had to "kiss Creed on the face." He'd tricked her into their first kiss that night, and she'd loved every second of it.

Pushing away the memories, she jammed a finger into his chest. "I don't need the walk down memory lane. You are going to stop manhandling me and stay away from me."

"Or what?" Creed challenged.

"Or I'll call security."

Creed smirked and folded those brawny arms across his perfect chest. "You know I can dismantle any security team."

Kiera huffed out a breath. "You leave me alone, or I'll kiss the blond guy on the face."

Creed's brows drew together, and his scowl was fierce. "Kiera," he warned. "Don't you dare disobey me."

"Disobey you?" Kiera laughed. "Watch me." She whirled and stomped away from him. He didn't follow. She didn't know if she was relieved or heartbroken all over again.

CHAPTER NINE

Kiera's righteous anger had carried her throughout the day. After she'd stomped away from Creed, she'd gone back to the cabana and lounged around next to William for an hour, praying Creed was watching. She hadn't gotten any glimpses of his glorious face or chest though, so she'd left to go try out the spa and reluctantly agreed to meet William at the steakhouse for dinner. Creed's warnings had only served to tick her off, but she knew she wouldn't be in danger, meeting William at a restaurant on the resort grounds.

She and William were settled into a corner table, the lighting so dim she could hardly make out the menu. Her mind wandered far away from the steakhouse.

Even the massage and facial at the spa this afternoon couldn't relax her or make her forget how it had felt when Creed had lifted her onto that bathroom counter, almost kissing her again. Why did he have to be such a hornet's nest, stirring her up and then stinging her again and again? Why couldn't she let him go?

He was only the love of her life, after all. She shook her head, biting at her cheek to keep from tearing up at all they'd lost.

"Is something wrong with the menu?" William asked.

"What? No." Kiera shook her head, her face flaming red.

"Oh. You looked upset."

The waiter came and set their drinks down then waited to take their dinner order.

Kiera ordered the salmon and broccoli then took a large drink of her piña colada daiquiri to cool the heat in her face. Her mouth puckered. She wasn't a drinker, but she thought this drink tasted off, like alcohol. Taking a small sip, she swished it around in her mouth then lifted the cup to her lips and discreetly spit it back out.

After William ordered, she said to the waiter, "Excuse me, this drink doesn't taste right. Can you please bring me a virgin?"

The waiter glanced at William. He gave him a nod and the man took her drink and scurried away. Kiera was feeling decidedly uncomfortable. What kind of old-school waiter looked to the man for a woman's confirmation on her drink? Why had she agreed to meet William here? To spite Creed would be the best answer. That was pretty stupid and immature of her. She didn't really like this guy, but Creed had made her so mad earlier. She had every desire to "disobey him." Who did the heart-breaking jerk think he was anyway?

The waiter brought her another daiquiri that tasted much better than the last one. She sipped it slowly and listened to William talk about himself again, something about his business. The man sure liked to prattle on. She responded just enough to keep William going, and let herself think about Creed and the way he'd looked in his swim trunks. Wowzas. How was a girl supposed to resist a man like that? She tamped down her attraction. She would resist him because he was a judgmental idiot who didn't love her. She wondered what kind of a job he was doing here. He'd told her he was in private security or some baloney at the gym. Why couldn't he even talk to her anymore?

A long time seemed to pass, and Kiera continued to sip her drink. Looking down, she was surprised that it was half gone, and her head felt like it was no longer attached to her body for some odd reason.

The waiter finally brought their salads, but Kiera wasn't hungry anymore. Her head was cloudy, and her stomach was swimming.

"All the other restaurants' service has been a lot quicker," Kiera said.

"I don't mind. I get to be with a beautiful woman longer," William said.

"Smooth talkerer." Kiera shook her head. Had her words just slurred? She felt like she was floating.

All the restaurants were open air with a roof to shelter from the rain or sun but no walls. Latin music floated in from the cabana outside of the steakhouse. She'd noticed couples dancing when she walked in, and a bar was close by. A lot of single men seemed to be hanging out at that bar. She swayed to the music, and William's eyes gleamed. He extended a hand. "Do you want to go dance before our meals come?"

Kiera accepted his hand, dancing was something she could do, and food didn't sound appealing right now. He pulled her to her feet, and she swayed. "Whoo. I'm a little unsteady tonight."

He chuckled. "Don't worry, beautiful. I'll hold you up." He wrapped his arm around her waist and pulled her in tight, escorting her through the restaurant, past the bar, and out to the dancing area.

They started dancing, and though her head was all out of whack and her body felt like it was floating, Kiera continued. It was more ingrained in her than walking.

Creed got notifications at close to the same time that Kiera and the duke had left their rooms. He forced himself to follow the duke. When Gunthry met up with Kiera at the dimly-lit steakhouse, Creed's stomach tumbled, and the muscles in his neck and arms tightened. By tomorrow night, River should be here with help. Could he really wait that long? He'd seen a few men lingering around or watching the duke at times, but he didn't think there were a dozen like Sutton feared. He could take them out, hogtie the duke and leave him in Kiera's spare bedroom until River got here. Then he could have Kiera all to himself. He almost smiled remembering her feisty response to him telling her not to disobey him. "Watch me." He had to admire her spice though there was nothing cute about the duke being that close to her. He should've told her exactly what Gunthry was capable of. It didn't matter that she'd ditched Creed and their love. Kiera still wouldn't run into this scum-bag's arms if she knew a hundredth of what he was capable of. Maybe she would do something smart tonight like go to the bathroom and Creed could intercept. If not, he might fail Sutton tonight if Gunthry tried anything on Kiera.

Time ticked by slowly as he sat at a low, almost hidden table in the darkened bar next to the restaurant and listened to the music from the dancing area and watched Kiera and the duke as they talked, sipped drinks, and waited for their food. He noted a few men in the shadows of the restaurant that he wanted to keep an eye on.

He turned his back to respond to the bartender, who had brought him another drink. The man had been quiet and discreet about Creed ordering coconut water in a martini glass. Of course, palming the guy a twenty hadn't hurt.

When he turned back around, Kiera and the duke were walking his direction. The duke's nasty hands were all over Kiera, and she was leaning heavily on him. Where were they going? They hadn't eaten. His protective instincts fired, and he knew he could take on whatever dozen men the duke had hidden if it meant protecting Kiera from going back to the slimeball's room. Would she really do that? Had she strayed so far from the girl Creed had dated and loved for eight years?

Creed couldn't think about it right now. He turned slightly as they approached him, but he was in deep shadow and neither of them looked his direction. They walked toward the dance floor and started dancing. Creed was glad he hadn't eaten, or he would've really been nauseated. How could she cling to the duke like that? The duke was grinning broadly as they danced much too close for Creed's liking. Kiera shouldn't be pressing herself against him. It was sickening. Creed's hackles rose, and he stood. He couldn't wait any longer.

As he strode toward them, he promised himself he would listen to Sutton. Somewhat. He wouldn't underestimate the duke, but when he killed the man with his bare hands, there wouldn't be anything left for his henchmen to protect.

Suddenly, Gunthry pulled a phone from his pocket, held it to his ear, and walked away from Kiera. Creed turned and pretended to be dancing with a couple who were bee-bopping around. They looked at him strangely, but he smiled and mouthed, "Sorry, one minute." That was all he needed.

The duke walked right behind him. Creed wanted to go grab Kiera right now, but he followed the duke slowly. The man crossed through the section of pools closest to the beach, talking on his phone the entire time. He entered the seventh building. It was where Gunthry's suite was so Creed hoped that he was going back to his room for some reason. A couple of well-built men followed Gunthry. Creed forced himself to wait until his phone buzzed, and he had confirmation of Gunthry entering his suite. Gunthry had better stay there if he wanted to see tomorrow.

Turning back, Creed saw a small grouping of men on the dance floor, and right in the middle of them, moving her beautiful body in a way nobody but Creed should ever see was … "Kiera." It came out as a growl, and now, nothing was holding him back. The duke may have left men to watch over his date, but Creed didn't care. He pushed off the concrete and sprinted across the short distance back to the dance floor.

The men were cheering and whistling and some of them were reaching out to touch her as Kiera danced, looking unsteady on her feet, which was something he'd never seen Kiera look. Creed burst through the circle, pushing two men out of his way and sending them sprawling to the ground.

"Kiera!" he yelled.

She turned to him, and her lip went out in a pout. Her eyes were cloudy, and she was definitely tipsy. What in the world? His Kiera didn't drink. Apparently, this new Kiera did.

One of the men he'd knocked down jumped up and launched himself at Creed. Creed grinned, lashed out with a side kick, and the man went flying. Someone came at him from behind and jumped onto his back. Creed whirled with the man clinging to his neck, and the man's legs flung out and struck two other guys.

Creed popped his head back, and the man screamed and flew off of him. He hit one dude with two jabs that downed him then put another in a chokehold and used him to take out the next guy who came at him. He had no clue if any of these losers were the duke's men or just idiots who wanted to ogle Kiera, but it felt so good to finally be fighting he didn't question it.

A roundhouse, a jab, two uppercuts, and a few well-placed kicks later and he had four men laying at his feet and others staring warily at him, some with future bruises, split lips, and bloody noses.

"You want to look at my girl some more?" He glowered at the men who were still standing. As one, they lifted their hands and backed away.

"She's all yours, buddy," one of the guys said.

Kiera swayed on her feet and looked about ready to collapse. She blinked up at him so trusting and full of love. "Creed?" she asked as if she hadn't seen him in months and didn't know that he was even in the same country.

Creed put a hand under her back and bent to put one under her legs. He swooped her off her feet and stormed through the crowd that had gathered to watch. No one stopped them. He rushed along a walkway parallel to the middle pool section but more in the shadows. If the duke came back, Creed didn't want him knowing who had taken Kiera. Luckily, the duke's men had tailed their boss.

Looking up at him, she touched his face and whispered, "You're really here."

"Of course I'm here."

Was she completely plastered? She was acting really off. Her breath smelled like sugar and alcohol, he'd watched her down a specialty drink, and she was acting like some of his high school buddies acted when they drank too much.

"I hated mighty Hawk for deserting me." She laid her head in the crook of his neck and sighed. "But you long-lost loved and came for me." Her words were slurred, and she wasn't making much sense. He hadn't deserted her. She'd betrayed him. He couldn't think about that right now. He made it to her elevator, the west end of the third building, and pushed the penthouse button with his elbow. They ascended the elevator with her still holding onto his neck, but she said nothing. Creed wondered if she had fallen asleep. Did Gunthry spike her drink or had she willingly consumed this much alcohol?

"I need your key, love," he said when they exited the elevator and arrived at her door.

Kiera stirred and pulled a key from her bra. Creed blew out a breath as he took it. He was going to have to fight hard to stay in control tonight, but there was no way he was kissing her when she was out of her head.

He slid the key over the look, and it clicked open. Cradling her close with one arm he maneuvered around and opened the door with his other hand. Setting the key on the counter, he walked into the dimly lit room and sank onto the couch with her in his arms. She settled against his chest like she belonged there. How he wished that were true.

He peered down at her. Her eyes were closed, and she was breathing evenly. "Kiera? Kiera?"

Her eyes slowly opened, and she gazed up at him. "Creed?" She smiled so sweetly, so happily. "You're here."

"I'm here, love." His watch and phone both buzzed, signaling the duke had left his room. Creed ignored the warning. He was ninety-nine percent sure the duke wouldn't vacate the property and disappear tonight. Kiera's safety was the new primary goal, and Creed wasn't leaving her right now. "Are you okay?"

"Don't feel so hot but is okay. You're here now."

Had Kiera changed so much that she would drink herself into this state or had the duke spiked her drink without her knowing? Why would Gunthry do that? Creed's jaw tightened. The why was too easy, the man planned to have his way with her. Creed was so done with this loser. He prayed nothing was keeping River because if someone didn't show up by tomorrow night, Creed was going to act without support and the duke would sorely regret coming onto Kiera.

Kiera released her hold on his neck and reached up, trailing her fingers along his cheek and then down along his neck. His stomach swirled with heat. She was too beautiful, too close. "My handsome Creed. My favorite man in the whole wide world," she drawled out. "You finally came back to me."

Creed nodded, his throat thickening. Was it possible that Kiera still loved him? She was out of her head right now, so he really couldn't let himself get too invested in what she was saying or the fact that he was holding her. Yet he had no plans of letting her go.

"Why don't you kiss me?" she asked, fluttering her eyelashes at him, and even though she wasn't herself, she was as alluring as ever. Creed slowed his breathing down. He remembered those months of imprisonment, being tortured and refusing to give them anything more than his rank.

He glanced over Kiera's beautiful face and body. The way she felt so soft yet firm in his arms. She wanted him to kiss her. How could resisting her be harder than holding his tongue through torture?

Creed shook his head. No matter how badly he wanted to kiss her, he couldn't allow himself to. He wouldn't kiss her when she was obviously drunk.

He gently pushed her head down to his chest and held her tight. "Why don't you rest?"

"I am tired." She wrapped her arms around his neck again and cuddled in. "We're the perfect fit, right?"

"Right." Creed took her words like a punch from Bridger to the gut. He and Kiera used to be the perfect fit. Now Kiera didn't seem to care about the love they once treasured. He wanted to savor holding her close like this, but it wasn't real, and it wasn't going to last. As soon as she slept off the alcohol that was in her system, she would give him her sassy attitude and pull away from him again. And he would let her because she wasn't his Kiera anymore. Not after what she'd done.

A loud rap came at the door. Kiera startled in his arms and looked at him with wide eyes. "Hello!" She called out much too loudly.

"Kiera?" It was the duke's voice, and Creed's stomach tightened. At least he didn't have to guess where Gunthry was. Kiera's loose tongue worried him though. She was likely to say anything. Then again, maybe he'd get the chance to kill the man right now.

"Hi!" Kiera yelled. "Sorry I can't get the door. I'm sleeping with—" Creed clamped his hand over her mouth and shook his head.

Kiera's eyes got even wider.

"Say you're going to bed. Don't tell him I'm here," Creed whispered, still holding her mouth tight.

"Kiera?" The duke called again. "Do I need to get some help?"

Kiera nodded slightly to Creed, looking like a little child who didn't understand anything that was going on. He removed his fingers.

"I don't feel well. I'm going to bed. I'll see you tomorrow." She practically screamed each sentence, and Creed thought if the duke hadn't been involved in getting her drunk and had a shred of decency, he probably would think she needed help.

"I could come sit with you."

"No." Kiera called out. "Good night!"

Creed put his finger over his lips and then carefully lifted her off of his lap and onto the sofa. He crept to the door and watched through the peep hole. The duke stood there for a few seconds. Then he signaled someone with his head and strode away. Creed made out a few shadows following him. He waited until they were in the elevator, and the door slid closed. Then he dead-bolted Kiera's door and brought a kitchen chair over to jam underneath it. Something wasn't right about the duke bringing his men to Kiera's door. If he wanted to sleep with her, wouldn't he come alone?

Creed tried not to overanalyze the duke's intentions. Losers like that probably did bring someone to watch over them at all times.

Kiera was sitting on the sofa with her head laid back against the cushions. He needed to hold her. He hoped he would be strong enough to resist her tonight. No. Creed would never. Under any circumstances. Never ever ever. There was no hope about it. It would be torture, but he wasn't doing more than putting an arm around her when she was drunk.

He waited a few more minutes until his phone and watch buzzed and he saw the duke enter his suite. Nobody went in with him. Did his men have rooms nearby? Creed would need to be more diligent tomorrow and figure that out.

Tonight, he planned to stay close to Kiera, unless fate really hated him and the duke left his suite again. Creed walked to the couch and bent down, lifting her into his arms. Her eyes fluttered open, and she said all delighted, "Creed! You didn't ditch me."

Creed pushed out a breath. They really needed to talk, but that wasn't happening tonight. He carried her into the master suite and settled her onto the mattress and pillows. Slipping her shoes off, he stared down at her. Her pale blue dress accentuated her beautiful brown skin and fit body. Her dark hair contrasted with the white pillow. How he wanted to simply run his fingers through it.

He turned to walk away, but Kiera's hand brushed his arm. "Please, don't leave me again."

Creed stopped. His tight rein on his self-control was slipping. He glanced back at her. She was staring at him steadily, almost as if she weren't out of her head. "Please, Creed."

His throat was too dry and tight to respond. He finally nodded.

She smiled and closed her eyes again. Creed slipped his shoes off and climbed onto the king bed next to her. She snuggled back against him, and he slid one arm under where the pillow met her neck and his other arm around her waist.

"Thank you for not deserting me again," she whispered. Then she sighed and seemed to drift off to sleep that quickly.

Deserting her? That hit low in the gut. He'd been captured and tortured, barely escaping with his life, and she called that desertion? She was delusional, rambling. He couldn't hold her accountable for anything tonight.

Creed didn't know if sleep would come. He cradled Kiera close and tried to shut his eyes, but he couldn't shut out the electrifying feeling of having her in his arms. It stirred something deep within him. He could easily admit the truth to himself—he loved her. If only she hadn't betrayed him and somehow thought he was the deserter. If only she truly loved him back.

CHAPTER TEN

Kiera woke with a pounding headache, rain slanting against the balcony windows, and scattered memories. She and William were sitting at the steakhouse, but they didn't eat anything. Then she was dancing with a bunch of men, and then Creed came in like a superhero and knocked a bunch of heads together before sweeping her into his arms and carrying her away, as if he were her knight in shining armor or something. She laughed derisively, but that hurt her head more.

"Good morning." Creed's voice carried over from the open doorway.

Kiera clutched the covers around her, but quickly realized she was still in her blue dress from last night. "What are you doing? Oh." She groaned, putting a hand to her head, talking hurt.

"Breakfast." He grinned and set a tray on the table by her bed. The scent of bacon and coffee was too much. "But first ..." He pulled out a small bottle of ibuprofen, popped the cap, and poured four into his palm. "Take these, and you'll start feeling better."

She took the pills with a swallow of water. Her stomach was churning, and food sounded awful. "What happened?"

"Well my first guess is *William*"—he said the name with such derision—"got you drunk."

"I don't drink," she said, laying her head back against the padded headboard and praying the ibuprofen kicked in soon.

"There are a lot of things I used to think you wouldn't do, but you've proven me wrong on those, now haven't you?"

Kiera straightened to cuss him out, but it hurt her head too much. She pressed her palm to her forehead, hoping to stay the pounding. "What are you talking about?"

Creed strode right up to the bed and placed a palm on each side of her hips. Kiera swallowed but couldn't swallow down the desire that rushed over her. Creed's hands had always been perfect, and she wanted him to hold her until all the pain went away.

"You let that loser get you drunk last night," Creed said slowly, as if she were slow. "What did you think he was planning to do with you?"

His words doused any intimacy she'd felt. Kiera glared at him, too out of sorts to slap or slug him, like he deserved. "I. Do. Not. Drink!" she yelled the last word. It was stupid of her, but her head didn't hurt nearly as badly as her heart did. Nothing could hurt as badly as having your heart gouged out by the man you loved. Why did Creed think so little of her? Thinking she'd allow herself to get drunk and then what? Did he really think she would sleep with that guy?

Creed gave a dry, humorless chuckle. "But you do other

things, don't you?" His eyes swept over her, but it wasn't in an I'm attracted to you way. It was derisive and mean.

"You'd better stop acting like I'm some floozy!" She pushed at his chest, but he didn't budge. Dang the man's muscled body.

"Stop playing the innocent victim, Kiera." He stood and paced away from the bed. "What in the world would possess you to meet that loser for dinner and then drink whatever he handed you?"

"I didn't take anything from him," she said as if Creed was the slow one. "Only directly from the waiter. I've heard the horror stories."

Creed ducked his chin and returned the you're-the-stupid-one stare.

"Wait. You think the waiter was in on drugging me?"

Creed shrugged, his eyes giving nothing away. She hated when he shut her out like some military guy. But that was what he was. Not her Creed anymore. A military hero who didn't need her and thought she'd ditched all her values. She knew he'd been through horrible things in his imprisonment, but the man she'd loved would never be so suspicious and derogatory.

"I thought I tasted alcohol in my first drink," she explained, though he didn't deserve an explanation. "So I asked for another one. It didn't taste like alcohol at all."

"They slipped some Everclear or a roofie in it then," he said. "Do you think that headache's just from dancing too much?"

Kiera acknowledged that with a chin lift, but terror raced through her. If Creed hadn't intervened last night, what horrors would she remember, or not remember, this morning?

Creed kept pacing then rounded on her again. "I'm glad to hear you didn't willingly let him get you drunk, but I hate that you would've willingly stayed the night with him."

Kiera sat up straight and gasped. "Oh! What would make you think that?"

"Why else would you go with that loser to dinner?"

"To tick you off!" she yelled.

His eyes widened, and then he grunted. "Well you're doing a beautiful job of that."

Kiera felt some satisfaction that he was as angry as she was, but her head was spinning instead of pounding now. Why did Creed think she was some hoochy mama who would sleep with a man she didn't know or like? They'd both fought hard to stay pure for each other for years. Did he really think she'd give all of that up because she became famous, because of the lies Milo spread, or because he'd died and he thought she'd gone crazy? She couldn't think of any other reasons why he would assume the worst of her. True, she'd had ample opportunities to turn her back on her values and maybe some smut magazine claimed she did, but she never had. His dying had devastated her, but she'd worked hard and focused on being the best dancer she could, being successful for him. Just like he'd asked her to in that letter. Now, she was regretting doing anything for this scuz-bucket.

"Did the fame get to you? Is that what it was? How did my Kiera become this?" He gestured at her.

"You need to leave," she said in the strongest tone she could muster up, so fed up with him, but still too out of sorts to push out of bed and push him out of her room. As if she could push him around even when she was in top physical condition.

Creed ignored her request. "Why are you working a resort in Mexico when you're one of the biggest stars in America? You could be on television, starring in your own show, on Broadway, in movies, anything you want."

Kiera looked down at the white comforter clenched between

her fingers, refusing to answer him. If the truth started spilling out, he'd know how desperately she'd loved him, how she still did. With as little as Creed seemed to think of her, her pride was all she had left, and she would cling to it with her French manicure for as long as she could.

Creed approached the bed, but she refused to look at him. He bent down close and tilted her chin up. "Kiera," he whispered, his dark gaze full of pleading. "What happened? Who took away your purity and confidence? Who did this to you?" He studied her, but she didn't answer. "Please tell me. I want to tear them apart for hurting you."

Their gazes locked. Kiera tried to wait him out but he wasn't backing down. As she looked into his eyes everything simplified. Though she loved him they could never be them again and he deserved to know how badly he'd devastated her.

She hurled at him. "You hurt me when you came back from the dead and never came for me. You're the reason I gave up. You're the one who ripped *me* apart." The words were torn from Kiera's lips but instead of making her feel better she felt empty and hollow.

Creed released her and straightened away from her. His gaze was full of angst and uncertainty. The muscles in his arms were all tight as he clenched his fists as if trying to control himself. "Oh, Kiera. Oh, love, no."

Kiera shook her head. He had no right to call her love. He'd destroyed her, and now, he was back at it again. Claiming she would've slept with William. Saying she was some loose woman.

Creed leaned toward her again, but then he pulled his phone from his pocket and straightened. "Excuse me. I have to take this. If it was anyone else ..."

"Take it. I don't care."

He backed away, but he was still focused on her. "This discussion isn't through. *We're* not through."

There he was. *The* Creed Hawk. Always in control. Always getting his way. Well, he wasn't going to get his way this time because she was done with the discussion and more than done with him. Somehow, she would ferret him out of her heart, and someday, she would be able to be happy again. If for no other reason than to prove she didn't need him.

Kiera simply glared at him. He strode into the living area, and she could hear him say in a harsh voice, "When are you coming?"

Kiera forced herself out of bed and slammed the door to her bedroom, clicking the lock. Not that locks would keep Creed out. She took a few gulps of the coffee. It scalded her throat, but the pain felt better than dealing with all the emotions Creed was tugging out of her. Grabbing a clean floral sundress, she rushed into her bathroom. Maybe a shower would clear her mind. Maybe then she could handle Creed. Maybe in her fantasies a lightning bolt from the rainstorm outside would strike Creed in the head and make him nice again.

"When are you coming?" Creed hated being tugged from Kiera right when the truth was finally coming out between them. If it wasn't Sutton on the phone, he would've simply ignored it. But Sutton would never call unless it was vital to the mission. Creed had to take it.

His mind was whirling though and far from Sutton or Gunthry. Could he forgive Kiera for giving herself to another man? She'd believed he was dead. He couldn't imagine how hard that would've been on her. It still shredded him to think of her in another man's arms, especially in another man's bed, but he had told her in that stupid Dear Jane letter to live her life, to move on. He had just never imagined she would move on that quickly and completely.

Yet he loved her, and he would forgive her if she would let him into her heart again. He would have forgiven her when he came for her that fateful day in Las Vegas if she'd shown the least bit of interest in him. If she'd even glanced his way when he called out to her.

"We resolved the issue, and I'm loading onto the Gulfstream now. I've got Corbin, Logan, and Cannon with me."

Creed felt the air rush out of him. River, Sutton, Corbin, Logan, and Cannon were coming. Plus, they would have Sutton's security guys and the MI6 men. Together, they could easily best Gunthry and any paid thugs he had. Then Creed would finally be free to get to the bottom of whatever Kiera had been trying to tell him. He prayed the two of them could somehow resolve their issues. "Thank you, sir."

"We might beat River and the MI6 guys there."

"I'll be happy to see any of you."

"Okay. Is Kiera all right?"

Creed could hear the shower going. At least she was feeling up to that. "The duke slipped something in her drink last night, either Everclear or a roofie because she didn't taste it."

Sutton pulled a quick breath in.

"But he took a phone call and left for his room, so I was able to get her back to her room and watch over her. I don't think he suspects anything, but maybe he does. He came to her room to check on her with several men in tow."

"With Gunthry, there's always something shady. Will she stay in her room today while you keep an eye on the duke?"

Disappointment shot through him. He wanted to talk with Kiera, not follow the idiot Gunthry around, but he recognized that he was on a job here, and if Gunthry snuck away while he was caught up in Kiera, that would be on him. He would keep Kiera safe and keep Gunthry in his sights until Sutton or River got here.

"I doubt she's going anywhere with the headache she has, and it's raining outside."

"Good. See you soon. Heart of a warrior."

"Heart of a warrior." Creed repeated their mantra.

The shower was still going. How long was she going to stay in there? Was she avoiding him? His phone and watch buzzed, and he clicked on his phone, watching as Gunthry strode out of his door, dressed in business casual. Dang it. He wasn't just strolling to the pool or spa dressed like that. He'd hoped the man would stay indoors with the bad weather and allow Creed to focus on Kiera.

Creed grabbed a notepad and pen from a side table and scrawled out a quick note for Kiera. He had to follow Gunthry. Thankfully, it would all be over soon. Then he could focus exactly where he wanted to—on Kiera.

CHAPTER ELEVEN

Kiera took her time showering, letting the warm water ease her aching head. By the time she dressed, brushed out her hair, applied some hair serum, and put on minimal makeup, she was feeling quite a bit better. The ibuprofen had apparently kicked in. She was also getting hungry, and she remembered that she hadn't had any dinner last night. Talking to Creed was more important than food, but she was scared. The way he seemed to perceive her—as some celebrity with loose morals who'd let stardom change her—made her fired up mad, but then she simply felt sad. Why would he think that of her? Could she convince him she wasn't like that? Did he love her enough to let go of whatever misperceptions he had and give them another chance? Was she willing to give him a chance after the way he'd deserted her after he came back from the dead and the way he'd treated her the past two days?

She sauntered into her bedroom and inhaled the delicious

scents of warm pancakes and crisp bacon. Opening her bedroom door, she scanned the main area. "Creed?"

All was quiet, and her stomach took a nosedive. Creed had left her? She looked into the extra bedroom and bathroom and saw he wasn't in there. Maybe he'd gone to shower or exercise and he'd be right back. She glanced around, at a loss, then spotted the note on the table.

Hurrying to the note, she picked it up. It was in Creed's scrawl but had been written so hurriedly it was almost illegible. *On a job. Be back tonight. William's dangerous. Don't leave your room.*

Kiera stared at the note incredulously. Once again, a job was more important than her. Her neck tightened with anger, but the rush of disappointment overshadowed the anger. She'd never been able to give up on Creed, loved him too much, but lately, all he seemed capable of was hurting her.

So he wanted her to sit around all day and wait for him like some sorry sass who had nothing better to do? The slight ache in her head, the overall feeling of yuckiness like she had the flu, and the fact that she wanted to stay far away from that William guy made her wander back into her room and sink down into a chair by the food. She started nibbling on some toast. Creed might get his wish for her not to leave her room, but only because she felt horrible, it was raining outside, and she didn't want to be exposed to William again. Hopefully, she'd be feeling better by this afternoon, and the rain would stop. She could go somewhere safe like the fitness center. At least make sure she left the room before Creed returned. Let him see how it felt to get ditched.

Creed crept after the duke, noting the two burly men following him as well. The three of them got in two separate taxis and left through the resort gates. Creed cursed. He hurried to the resort's circle drive. Luckily, several taxis were waiting. He jumped into one and said, "Follow that taxi. The white one with the green stripe." The duke's men had gotten into a white taxi with a pink stripe. Fortunately, both were easily identifiable.

"Si, señor."

They drove along the heavily-wooded main road that ran north and south. There was enough traffic Creed didn't think he looked conspicuous following them. The heavy rain also helped. The taxis stayed together and, within minutes, pulled into an industrial park of sorts. There weren't any gates or guards, and it was busy with lots of vehicles and equipment operators moving around. A yellow taxi, like the one Creed was in, would be pretty conspicuous.

"Keep follow?" the man asked.

"No. Drive past until we're covered by the trees then stop."

The man obeyed. "We wait?"

"For a moment. Gracias." Creed was trying to decide if he should sneak into the area on foot and see what the duke was up to or just wait for him to reappear. He waited because his only job was to make sure the duke didn't disappear. Since there was no beach access, helicopters, or planes, he didn't think the duke was leaving the island from here.

About twenty minutes passed before the two taxis exited the industrial park and headed back the way they'd originally come.

"Go," Creed said. "Follow the taxis again."

"Si." The man flipped a U and almost took out a scooter coming the other way. Creed couldn't imagine being on a scooter in this rain, but then, he'd survived the Philippines as part of a

Navy deployment, and they were almost always out in the elements. He had sworn he would never dry out again.

The taxis headed back through the resort's gates. Creed's taxi waited as the others got clearance to go in. Then his taxi pulled up to the security building. A guard took his room number and name and checked it against the picture they'd taken of him the day he checked in before his taxi was gestured through. The duke and his men had already exited their taxis, and he could see them through the large windows of the main front building of the resort.

He paid his driver and climbed out into the rain. Was his luck changing? Maybe Gunthry had done what business he had and would hunker down in his room the rest of the day. If that little miracle happened, Creed would finally be able to talk to Kiera.

Creed followed them until the three men entered the Italian restaurant and settled in for lunch. He stood in an alcove that sheltered him from some of the rain, but the rain was coming down sideways now. He sighed. It was going to be a long, wet day.

CHAPTER TWELVE

Kiera progressively felt better physically as the day full of rain and nothingness wore on. She didn't feel good enough to go workout, and she didn't really fancy sitting in a restaurant by herself, going to the spa, or risking an encounter with William, so she'd spent the day reading and being lazy and waiting. Sadly, her emotional state hadn't improved. She was sick and tired of Creed bossing her around, especially when he seemed to think so low of her and not care about her. Part of her wanted to leave her room and find some place out of the rain to hang out so when he came back he'd feel half as awful as she did. Part of her wanted to wait right here so when he returned she could give him a piece of her mind.

A soft rap came on her door late afternoon. It had dang well better be Creed. It seemed she'd been waiting for this man her entire life.

"Kiera?" It was him.

She walked to the door and looked through the peephole at

him, admiring the way he looked with his clothes clinging to him from the rain. "Yes?" she called.

"Let me in please."

"Yeah. I'm gonna have to take a raincheck on that one." She smiled when he pressed up closer to the peephole.

"Let me in. Now."

"Not happening." Her hackles rose. "I am *not* spending my life waiting around for you, Creed Hawk."

Creed's face softened, and though it was distorted by the peephole, he was still so handsome to her. "I'm sorry I had to leave," he said just loudly enough for her to hear him.

That hit her square in the chest. Creed wasn't one to throw around apologies. When he did admit he was in the wrong, he really and truly meant it. He was sorry for leaving—just for today or for the times he'd had to leave her in the past? Did she dare let him in and risk her heart being broken all over again? Would he want to talk, explain why he'd left her when he came back from the dead? Left her without any explanation? What would he say about her giving up her hard-earned career and fame after he ditched her and devastated her, taking away her will to fight and succeed?

"Please let me in, love."

The sorry, please, and love were pushing her to give in.

"What incentive do I have?" She bit at her lip. Things were pretty heavy between them, yet she couldn't resist teasing him. He'd asked her that same question years ago when she told him she would teach him how to dance. He'd given her that charming grin of his and claimed he didn't want to learn to dance and asked what incentive he had. She'd told him he could teach her how to really kiss after she taught him how to really dance. They'd already kissed a few times before that night, but that night the dancing and the kissing had been magical.

Creed chuckled, and she could see his taut muscles relax. He must've been clenching his fists pretty tightly. "I'll teach you how to really dance," he said.

Kiera laughed too. She wanted to swing the door wide and kiss him on the face, but she waited, making herself count to ten. She pressed her eye to the keyhole and could see Creed staring at the door, waiting and waiting. Finally, she couldn't stand it any longer. She undid the deadbolt and flung the door wide.

Creed straightened. With his wet shirt clinging to his well-muscled body and droplets of water glistening in his hair and on his face, he was nothing short of glorious.

"Hi," she said. It came out shy and too quiet.

Creed's gaze swept over her, and they simply studied each other for half a beat. Then he strode across the gap, shutting the door with a resounding bang, and swept her off her feet, crushing her against his chest.

Her sundress got damp from the wetness of his shirt. He smelled like fresh rain and his distinctive Burberry cologne. Kiera stared up into his handsome face as he studied her hungrily. "Hi," she whispered again.

A smile flitted across his face, but it was there and gone quickly. "No more goodbyes," he said.

The words rang through her head, and she loved them. They still had so much garbage to resolve it would overflow a landfill, but if Creed would promise no more goodbyes, she would deal with any refuse the past had dealt them.

Creed bowed his head and captured her lips with his own. The kiss was hungry and filled with longing and too much time lost. Kiera clasped her hands tightly around his muscular back and held on as they danced with only their lips.

He pulled back and moaned. "Kiera, I've missed you." Then he was kissing her again, and it was more intense and all-encompassing than any kiss she'd ever experienced, even with Creed. His hands framed her face, and she ran her hands up his back, across his shoulders and down to his biceps where she clung to the solid muscle to try and stabilize herself. Her head was even cloudier than it'd been when she was drugged last night.

Creed finally slowed down the kisses and tenderly kissed her cheek and then her brow before simply holding her close.

When Kiera was able to form words, she teased him, "I thought you were going to teach me how to dance."

Creed chuckled. "That was better than any dance."

Kiera laughed, and even as a professional, lifelong dancer, she had to agree with him.

"But if you insist." Creed winked and took her hand, placing his other hand at her hip. He waltzed her slowly around the small living area, twirled her out and in a few times and then dipped her low, kissing her. The dance was sweet, and the kiss even sweeter.

Creed pulled her upright and in tight to his chest as they gently swayed together, no music, just them. Creed's stomach grumbled, and Kiera laughed. "Hungry?"

"I didn't get any breakfast, or dinner last night, come to think of it. Too worried about my girl."

His girl? "It's almost time for dinner again," she said. "Do you want to ..." For some reason, she was feeling shy again, like she was the sophomore asking the hottest senior boy to the girl's choice dance. She'd done that all those years ago, and Creed had said yes. "Go to dinner?"

Creed's gaze swept over her face. "Would you be opposed to ordering room service? I hate to interrupt the dancing, and especially the kissing, but we really need to talk."

Kiera nodded, realizing he was right. They broke apart, and she got him a towel to dry his hair and sit on while he ordered a bunch of food and drinks from the room service menu. Finally, they sat side by side on the couch. Creed took her hand and matched their palms together then intertwined their fingers. His hand was so much bigger than hers. She'd always thought her darker skin and smaller hand looked perfect in his manly grasp.

"I'm not even sure where to start," he said.

Kiera turned slightly so she could see his face. "It's okay, Creed. We can work through this. I can forgive you."

Creed's eyebrows shot up. "You can forgive *me*?"

All of the ardor she'd been feeling for him evaporated with that one inflection. She wrenched her hand free, shot to her feet, and glared at him. "What grievous sin have I committed? You act like I'm the one in the wrong when the truth is you deserted me! You ditched me and broke my heart, and I fell apart. Yet, for some reason, you act like *you* need to forgive *me*." She placed a hand on her chest and didn't even care that her voice was full of venom.

Creed stood and faced her. They were half a foot away, but it felt like miles. "Kiera," he said softly. "You and I ... we made promises. We stayed strong for each other, for our wedding night."

Kiera was so confused right now. Where had he gotten the misinformation that she was a floozy? Creed would never believe the rumors Milo had started. "Yeah."

"When you broke those promises, it broke my heart."

"I broke what?" She practically yelled the last word. Maybe

he believed the rumors because of what she'd said the last night thy were together. Forcing herself to lower her voice she said, "What are you talking about? You're upset because of that last night before you were deployed, when I tried to get you to do more and you were the strong one? You think because of that I turned into some loose woman?"

Creed opened his mouth, but she talked over him. "I've got news for you, mister. You aren't some holier than thou saint. There were many times throughout high school and college that I was the strong one, the one who stopped *you* from going too far!" She started ticking them off. "Senior ball, the night on the beach after you graduated college, the time you came back from leave after your first deployment." She'd listed enough, though there were more.

Creed stared at her as she finished her tirade. "Are you done?"

"I shouldn't be, but I'll allow you to speak, you two-faced jack-tard." How could he believe because of what she'd said that night that she'd ditch all of their morals? He'd never even acted upset that night. He'd laughed about it and reassured her they would be together.

Creed cracked a smile but sobered quickly. "I'm not talking about that night."

"Then what are you talking about?"

"I'm talking about how hard we both fought to stay pure and you threw it all away with that Milo joker."

"Milo?" Kiera's eyebrows rose along with her temper. So he did believe the rumors? How could he believe that crap, without so much as asking her? His family had plenty of media exposure and he knew as well as anybody how reporters twisted the facts? "You think I slept with Milo?"

Creed folded his arms across his chest and looked down at her all supercilious. "He moved in with you for three weeks before I came back from being captured. Are you claiming you lived together, but it was platonic?" His arched eyebrow mocked and angered her even more.

"I *never* lived with Milo."

Creed's brow furrowed. "What? Sutton told me that Milo's agent confirmed all the rumors that you two were together. He had pictures of you two together but also of Milo leaving your condo early in the morning and late at night."

"Those pictures were probably taken when Milo knocked on my door at all hours and I asked him to leave. I don't know who this Sutton joker is or where they got doctored pictures that looked like we were together, but I know Milo's agent and the *only* thing he cares about is getting Milo bigger contracts and more publicity, no matter who it hurts."

Creed shook his head, not budging in his judgmental superiority. "Sutton's information is always correct."

"Not this time." Kiera poked him in the chest. "Milo and I were dance partners, nothing more, nothing less. He kissed me when I was miserable and alone and thought you were dead and all it did was make me angry." She gulped, remembering how horrific that time had been. "I always told him we could only be friends because I felt nothing for him. Even when you were *dead*, I saved myself for you, Creed."

Creed studied her for half a second. Then his jaw sort of dropped open, and he quickly snapped it shut. "The Kiera I know would never lie," he whispered.

"That's right." She thrust out her hip and glared at him. "I don't drink. I don't lie. And I definitely don't sleep around, you supercilious cretin."

Creed chuckled, and then he whooped and picked her up off her feet. He kissed her, devouring her mouth with his and didn't set her down until a loud rap came at the door.

Creed gently put her feet on the ground and gave her one more tender peck. "To be continued," he said.

Kiera tilted her head to the side. "We'll see. I told you not to manhandle me and you still have a lot of explaining to do."

Creed smiled. "I'll talk all night if I can manhandle you some more."

Kiera smiled and said sassily, "Maybe you'll be that lucky. You're still in trouble in my book."

Creed laughed then checked the peep hole before opening the door. The young man brought in the trays of food. Creed tipped him and thanked him, walking him out. They uncovered the dishes, and Creed started cutting into a bite of salmon. It was obvious he was starving. Kiera watched him eat, slightly in awe at how ravenous he was. He still had impeccable manners though. He was a Hawk after all, but she was amazed at how quickly he could chew, swallow, and repeat.

"Your mom would not appreciate your food consumption speed right now." She teased him.

Creed sat back and wiped at his mouth with a napkin. "Sorry. I learned to devour food in the SEALs, especially in Syria when I was sure I would starve to death." His eyes traveled over her. "I would rather devour your lips."

Kiera laughed though she hated thinking about him imprisoned and starved. "Eat. Maybe you'll get a sample of my lips later."

Creed winked and filled his plate again. Kiera loaded a small sampling of many of the dishes onto her plate and started eating. She ate a little bit but mostly toyed with her food and watched

Creed eat. Finally, she asked, "So this Sutton guy told you I was living with Milo, and you didn't think to come ask me?"

Creed stopped eating, drank a long swallow of water and then answered. "As soon as I could get my mom to stop clinging to me after we were released, I told my family I wanted to go to Vegas. Callum offered his fastest jet and his pilot. All I wanted to do was find you."

Kiera's heart was beating so high and fast, she felt like it was in her throat. He had come for her.

"When I got to the Bellagio, I found the hallway where your dressing room was. The security guards wouldn't let me through, so I was ... dismantling them." He gave her an embarrassed grin, but his grin disappeared. "Then I saw you and that Milo guy. He was hugging you and then kissing you. It about killed me."

Kiera put her hand over her mouth. "You were the guy the security guards were tackling in the hallway the night I found out you were alive. You called my name."

"Yes." He nodded. "All the fight went out of me when I saw you kissing him. Sutton came for me in the security office a couple hours later and told me that you'd been with Milo for months and living with him for three weeks. I thought ..." His voice dropped and came out gravelly and painful. "I thought you'd"—he swallowed—"been with him. I thought you'd betrayed our love, betrayed me, and all that not long after I'd supposedly died."

Kiera couldn't speak. She was sick.

"I knew it would've been awful for you thinking I was dead, but I still couldn't stand the thought of you not loving me, our memories, enough to keep yourself pure for marriage. Even if that marriage wasn't to me." He splayed his hands. "So I went to work for Sutton and kept myself busy and tried not to think about you." He smiled sadly. "It didn't work. Though I was angry at you for what I'd thought you'd done. I never stopped loving you."

Kiera couldn't stand not touching him right now. She scooted over to him and plopped herself on his lap, wrapping her hands around his neck. "I need to kiss you on the face right now."

Creed chuckled. "Just a second." He grabbed a mint off the tray and tossed it in his mouth. "Okay, now."

Kiera laughed and kissed him and kissed him. An explosion of happiness rushed through her. It was like coming home yet more exciting than Christmas morning. His lips were tender and firm, and she was warm from head to toe.

When she pulled back, her eyes feasted on his handsome face. The face she'd always loved. "As soon as my mama called and said you were alive, I caught a red-eye from Vegas and headed straight for Long Island. When I got there, your mom told me that you'd already left with some 'handsome English man,' and I thought you'd ditched me. Oh, Creed. Of all the stupid misunderstandings. How could you think I wouldn't wait for you?"

Creed buried his head in her chest and let out a groan of pain. "I'm sorry. Kiera, please forgive me. I was blind and stupid, and you deserve so much more."

Kiera grasped his cheeks with her hands and pulled him up so she could look at him. "I love you, Creed. Of course, I forgive you."

Creed pulled her in tight and kissed her. Kiera was certain she'd found heaven, and she was never letting anything come between them again.

CHAPTER THIRTEEN

As Creed held Kiera close, he wondered if he'd ever been this happy. Kiera had always made him happy. The pain of what he'd gone through—being captured, imprisoned, and tortured, and then thinking the reason he made it through all of that had been disloyal to him had nearly destroyed him. It made this moment of happiness even more meaningful.

There was also the sweet realization that he and Kiera's time was now. Before, he'd known he would have to leave, to fulfill his calling to be a SEAL, but he'd completed that mission. Now, even if he kept working for Sutton, his focus could be Kiera.

"Do you ever think about why?" she murmured into his chest.

"Yeah. All the time. The imprisonment was ... I really can't talk about it, but complete misery doesn't even come close. I wondered many times why we had to go through that, be separated with you thinking I was dead. But I do know it makes moments like this all the better." He ran his hands over her trim waist and was so happy to hold her close.

"I can't even imagine. The thought of you being tortured"—she shuddered—"starving, miserable."

"Yeah, let's not dwell on it."

"You're so tough." She glanced up at him with her beautiful dark eyes wide. "If I went through something like that, I'd want to go on talk shows, write a book about it, have everybody know how bad it was and give me lots of pity."

Creed chuckled, but any mirth fled quickly. "You say that, but truly, I pray several times a day for the Lord to just help me forgive and forget."

She nodded, considering. "Sometimes, I take the why a step further. Sometimes, I wonder why you ever had to choose your path. Why you ever had to leave me." She bit at her lip and looked so kissable in her humble questioning it was all he could do to stay his mouth. "Sorry, that's so selfish and petty of me."

"No, it's not," he hurried to reassure her. "I hated leaving you, my mom, and my brothers, but I knew from the time I was little that I'd be a SEAL. I knew it. For me, it was a calling from God just as surely as someone called to a ministry or a mission. Does that make sense?"

She nodded. "I know that about you. How honorable and good you are to want to serve, to protect. Sorry, sometimes I just get bratty."

"You are the farthest thing from bratty." He let himself kiss her and got distracted for many minutes with her perfect lips.

When he pulled back, she glanced up at him, and her eyes were glistening. "You know when I was teasing you in the gym? About your brothers?"

He remembered. She'd been mad at him, but her teasing had

actually been cute. Still, he didn't like being compared to his brothers. They all had their own paths, and he was proud of each of their successes.

"I think your path in life is the noblest, Creed."

He smiled. "That means a lot. Thank you." He paused. "I think my brothers are the greatest. I love that we all have our own paths."

"The great Hawk brothers. All famous in their own right." She teased him.

He chuckled. He loved his family, but their life wasn't cake and roses. People assumed because they were wealthy and talented they had it easy, but every one of his brothers worked hard to succeed. To try to live up to their father's expectations. They worked harder than most people he knew, truly. "We didn't have any choice not to be successful."

"Because of your dad?"

"Yeah. You remember how it was. Mom adored us and thought we could do no wrong. We all worked hard to prove her right. Dad tolerated us, for Mom, and if any of us messed up, he would've been so disappointed in us." He trailed his hands along her back remembering. "BUDs training was much worse than I could've foreseen, and so many guys rang the bell. But no matter how bad it got, even when I thought they were going to drown or kill me with training, I remembered my dad telling me if I ever quit, it would disappoint him and break my mom's heart. I couldn't do either."

"I don't really like your dad." She admitted.

Creed laughed. "No one does. Except maybe my mom. Even Callum doesn't really like him, though it seems like he's becoming just like him. Bridger loved to call my dad Tomahawk."

"Bridger got away with a lot more than any of the rest of you."

"That's for sure."

He trailed his hand up her neck and cupped her face. "Why are we wasting this time talking about my dad and brothers when we could be kissing?"

Kiera giggled so cutely, but he cut it off by pressing his lips to hers. Much, much later, he pulled back. "I really need to go take a shower and put some clean clothes on." His clothes were still damp from being out in the rain for so long, and he was afraid he smelled like wet dog. The duke and his men had lingered over lunch for hours before going on a long walk in the rain down to the ferry dock and along a huge wooden pier next to the resort. Creed wished he knew what they were looking for, what they were planning. River or Sutton should be here within hours, so he tried not to worry too much about the duke. Finally, the men had returned to their rooms, almost as wet as Creed. Thankfully, he hadn't gotten any notice that the duke had left his room tonight.

"Will you be okay without me for a few minutes?" he asked.

Kiera sighed dramatically. "If I must. But hurry."

He kissed her and headed for the door. "Deadbolt this behind me. The job I'm on is tracking that William idiot. He's an escaped convict with quite the past."

Kiera's eyes widened. "That's why you had to leave earlier, to track him?"

"Yeah, but he's been in his suite all evening working on his computer. Sutton and his other men will be here soon with MI6 to apprehend him. I just have to keep an eye on him for a little while longer." He kissed her slowly, savoring it. "But you're much more important. If I have to go follow him again, I want to know that you're safe."

Kiera nodded. "I'll stay in my room with my deadbolt turned and pepper spray in hand."

He chuckled. "Good girl. I'll see you soon." He slipped out of her door and waited to hear the deadbolt click. He'd hurry through his shower and be back by her side soon. He prayed the duke would sit in his room until Sutton or River got here and apprehended him. Before, Creed had wanted to dismantle the man. Now, all he wanted was to be with Kiera. As soon as the duke was under arrest, Creed was going to spend as long as Kiera wanted at this beautiful resort, with her by his side. Afterwards, they would go home, be with their families, let their moms plan the dream wedding. Unless ... could he talk Kiera into eloping?

Chuckling, he waited impatiently for the elevator, not wanting to be away from Kiera one second longer than he needed to.

Creed hurried to his room in building twelve, up to the tenth floor, and through his shower. His watch beeped when he was rinsing off. Wiping his face clean, he checked it quickly and cursed. The duke was on the move. At least Kiera was safe in her room. Any time now, Sutton or River would be here and this job would be done.

CHAPTER FOURTEEN

Kiera didn't like the silence and loneliness that crept in as soon as Creed left. She turned on the television and tried to distract herself, but it didn't work. Stacking all the room service dishes, she opened the door and set the trays outside where they would pick them up. As she bent down, arms came around her waist and painfully jerked her to her feet.

She whirled and saw William glowering at her. She screamed, but a hand covered her mouth, and somebody behind her held her tightly while someone else ripped her hands behind her back and tied them up. Kiera couldn't even squirm with whoever was restraining her holding her.

William smiled. "You should've just stayed with me last night. You would already be on your way to your new life."

Kiera glared at him, though chills of terror raced through her. What was he talking about?

The hand was removed from her mouth. She screamed out,

but duct tape was slapped onto her mouth so quick she barely got a squeak out.

William trailed a hand down her cheek. She tried to move her face, but the men held her tight. "So beautiful and famous. You'll make me a lot of money, sweetheart." He inclined his head. "Let's go."

Kiera was plucked clean off her feet and thrown over some guy's shoulder. Instead of the elevator, they threw open the door for the stairs and pounded down them. Kiera was jostled and banged around. Her stomach was tumbling and her head full of fear and confusion. It sounded like William hadn't drugged her last night so he could have his way with her. It sounded like he was planning to sell her. Icy terror ran down her spine. Kiera squeezed her eyes shut tight and started to pray.

Creed rushed out of his room and knew he had limited time to find the duke. The duke could easily disappear with the time it took Creed to get dressed after his shower, and the elevator had been unbelievably slow. He searched around the main areas for a few minutes but didn't see the duke. An uneasy feeling settled in his gut. He needed to know where Gunthry was and stick to him until River or Sutton got there. He wanted this job done in the worst way. He glanced up at where he knew Kiera's penthouse suite was across the huge complex of rooms. Her lights were still glowing softly. How he wanted to be there with her. Sadly, now was not that time.

Heading for the main building, he said to the front desk attendant. "I need the head of security, right now."

She blinked at him but grabbed a phone and dialed. Within

half a minute, a burly well-dressed Mexican man strode up to him. "How can I help you, señor?"

"I need to look at your security film for the past ten minutes."

"I'm sorry, sir."

"I'm not asking." Creed pulled out his credentials as a private investigator and one of Sutton Smith's men.

The man's eyebrows went up.

"You've heard of Sutton Smith?"

"Si, señor."

"Security film?"

"This way."

Creed rushed after the man, praying Gunthry hadn't vacated the property. As they walked in, two men straightened quickly and hid their phones that they'd obviously been playing on. The head of security arched an eyebrow at Creed but didn't reprimand his men in front of him.

The security room was impressive with up-to-date equipment and huge screens. Creed had them scroll back through the footage outside of Gunthry's rooms. Sure enough, thirteen minutes ago he exited his room and took the elevator. They followed him across the property, three large men trailing him, and then up the elevator to the outside of Kiera's suite. Creed's stomach dropped. They fast-forwarded through. The film showed them waiting outside Kiera's door for four minutes and twenty-nine seconds.

Creed watched in horror as Kiera opened the door and stacked trays of food on the ground. One man grabbed her and another man bound her hands. They put duct tape on her mouth then headed for the stairs. Creed could barely stand still as they quickly went through the film and showed them exiting at the main level and heading toward the pools. Less than one minute ago it showed them hurrying toward the beach. Creed thought of Gunthry checking out the ferry dock and the pier earlier today and his body filled with dread.

"Tell your men to look on the beach, the ferry dock, or the pier for them," Creed yelled as he took off at a run out of the security office, not waiting for their confirmation.

He was halfway across the second set of pool decks when his phone rang. He yanked it out and kept sprinting. "Hello." He gasped out.

"Creed, it's River. I'm here. I can't believe you're getting paid to—"

"Head for the beach," he yelled out. "The duke's got Kiera."

Creed shoved his phone back into his pocket. River would be exactly the backup he needed, but the duke could already be gone. If they left by boat, would Creed ever find Kiera? There was a big ocean out there.

Creed should've realized Gunthry wouldn't give up on having Kiera after his stunt last night. He pushed his legs to rotate faster, but his stomach churned quicker than his legs. Why had Creed ever left her side?

CHAPTER FIFTEEN

Kiera bounced against some burly guy's shoulder as the men ran along the beach and then down a long wooden pier. The rain was still coming down, and within seconds, she was drenched. They made it to the end, and the man set her on her feet but kept his arm around her. The pier widened into a large covered dock. The rain splattered against the covering, and waves lapped gently against the side of the pier. The wind was warm, but as wet and terrified as she was, Kiera's entire body was trembling.

She heard William cursing and yelling at one of his men. "Where's the boat? Where are the other men with my merchandise?"

"Don't worry so much, señor. Is all coming."

William backhanded the man who was twice his size. "Speak again, and I'll kill you." He threatened in a low growl.

The man held up his hands and backed away, running into Kiera and the man holding her. The rain made the late evening sky as dark as midnight. Kiera peered out into the ocean and saw lights headed their way. It looked to be a decent-sized boat, a small yacht. If they got her on that boat, they could take her anywhere. She looked down at the dark water below, with the rain splattering on it. Could she keep herself afloat without her hands? She'd have to wait for just the right moment. Her heart was racing, and with the duct tape over her mouth, she felt like she was forcing oxygen in and out of her nose too quickly. She couldn't pass out before she had a chance to escape. She tried to look back down the dock, but the man holding her prevented her from seeing that direction.

The boat came closer and closer. The men were all focused on its approach. The dock was open with no railings. Kiera waited until the yacht bumped against the dock and the men tied it off. William strode onto the low rear platform and open deck of the yacht, yelling at someone else. The man holding her started to pick her up. Kiera threw her head back as hard as she could and felt the back of her head make impact with his face. He cried out, and his grip loosened. She flung her body toward the water, and then she was falling.

The warm water embraced her and closed over her head. Kiera sank for half a second before kicking furiously, trying to angle away from the boat. Her head broke the surface, and she snorted through her nose, trying to get enough air in. She could hear men's voices shouting and chaos above her as she kicked for all she was worth back toward the beach. Maybe the cover of darkness and the rain would help her get away. Maybe someone had seen them and would come help? Maybe a miracle would happen and Creed would find her. If she didn't drown first.

Kiera tired quickly, and her head slipped under water. She rolled over onto her back and kept kicking as ferociously as she could, ignoring the yells and the fear pounding through her head.

It was too hard to keep afloat with her arms tied, even floating on her back. A wave covered her face and filled her nose. With the duct tape over her mouth, she couldn't gasp for air. She lifted her head and tried to push air and the salt water out of her nose and pull oxygen in, but she wasn't getting enough.

Breathe, in and out, she told herself, but it was hard to settle down and even harder to get enough oxygen and keep her head above the water. She kicked harder, and her leg cramped. She slipped under the water, but she ignored the pain and kept kicking until her head popped up again.

A light blinded her, and she screamed against the duct tape as a huge body launched into the water next to her. Within seconds, the man reached her side and roughly grasped her. She tried to kick at him but only succeeded in going underwater and catching a noseful of salt water. He pushed her toward the boat and hands grasped her and yanked her onto the yacht's rear platform.

"Stupid girl." William backhanded her, and she tasted blood. He bent down in her face. "You're going to pay for that." He sneered and pointed at all the men circling him. "I'll let you use your imagination as to how."

Kiera screamed against the duct tape, but hardly any sound escaped. Her heart was thumping out of control, and salt water stung her eyes. It was hard to get enough oxygen through her nose, but she concentrated on inhaling and exhaling so she wouldn't pass out. She prayed desperately for help, but it didn't look like any help was coming.

William grasped her shoulders and squeezed until she thought her bones would crack. Kiera struggled to free herself but couldn't. She glared at him, no matter what she wouldn't submit to these men.

He shoved her down to the smooth floor of the boat. Kiera couldn't catch herself with her hands bound and her head slammed against the surface. She cried out, curling in a ball to protect herself but William left her alone.

The bright spotlight highlighted the dock and the ocean around them. Kiera blinked bleary eyes. She could see shadows sprinting down the dock. Dark, large shadows. More of William's men, or did she dare hope for help? She prayed desperately.

"Joe should be here by now with the other women," William muttered.

"Si." A man answered.

"He's got one more minute. Then we're leaving. Cut that light," William commanded.

The night around them went dark again. Only the soft lights of the yacht tried to penetrate the dark rain. Kiera blinked through the rain. Her wet hair hung into her eyes. She shivered more from fear than cold.

The footsteps came first, and then men appeared.

"Joe?" Someone called out.

"You wish."

Kiera's eyes widened as Creed leapt onto the yacht deck, plowing into William. William squealed like a pig as his head slammed into the hard floor of the boat. Then chaos erupted. Another large man with Creed was fighting two guys at once. She saw three more fights going on. From what she could tell, Creed and his buddies were sorely outnumbered. Hope fluttered in her chest but she knew their chances of success were slim. She'd already lost Creed once and it about devastated her. If Creed was killed trying to save her she'd rather die herself.

She watched Creed knock William around, punching him

repeatedly until William stopped resisting. Then Creed jumped to his feet and started fighting someone else. One fight got close to her, and she kicked out at the man she'd seen with William, connecting with his ankle. He fell to the dock, and the tall guy fighting him dove on top of him and pummeled him. When she was sure the man had to be unconscious, the guy stopped hitting him and turned to Kiera. "Thanks."

Kiera hoped he'd loosen her bonds or take off the duct tape from her mouth, but he sprang back into another fight. Another group of men arrived at the end of the dock, carrying several women who were bound like Kiera. Kiera tried to scream to warn Creed, but the men dumped the women on the dock and jumped into the fray on the yacht's open deck.

William rose unsteadily to his feet. Kiera cried into the duct tape when she saw a gun in his palm. Creed was fighting a huge man, trading hit after hit, and was oblivious to the threat. Kiera's heart threatened to explode out of her chest as she pushed awkwardly to her feet and ran across the smooth boat deck, trying to reach William before he killed Creed. William pointed the gun straight at Creed, a sadistic smile on his face.

A weapon fired, and Kiera yelled against her mask. Creed whirled around, and Kiera's body sagged against a nearby chair. Creed hadn't been hit. Who had? The fighting stopped temporarily as everyone seemed to be wondering the same thing. Kiera finally found the victim in the gloomy rain illuminated by the yacht's soft lights. William was splayed out, blood running down his forehead. Her stomach pitched at seeing someone dead right before her eyes, but she couldn't find any remorse in her for William.

"We were supposed to apprehend him," a regal voice said from the darkness of the dock.

"It was classic self-defense, or defense of my buddy Creed. However you want to spin it to the authorities."

"Sure, Corbin, whatever you say." Another man slapped him on the back.

Six more men walked into the light from the boat. They were all well-built and obviously knew their way around a fight. One man was older than the others but still fit and reminded her of James Bond. He inclined his chin to Creed. "Sorry we missed the party."

The men around him all aimed weapons at the men who'd been with William. They held up their hands and didn't look like they would put up anymore resistance.

Creed pushed out a breath and gave them a shaky grin. "You missed out. It was a good one."

Another man in a suit, who looked more like a government worker rather than military like the rest of them, shook his head. "Guess we don't have to worry about extracting the criminal back to British soil."

"I'd bury him here," the older man said. "Maybe just throw his ugly carcass in the ocean."

Creed pushed around men until he was at Kiera's side and pulled her into his arms. She felt someone cut her hands free, and that was all she needed. She wrapped them around Creed's back and held on tight.

Creed pulled back slightly. "This is going to hurt, love."

She nodded, wanting the stupid tape off, no matter how badly it hurt. Creed gently held on to her cheek and pried the edge of the tape up then ripped it off. She cried out as it tugged at the tender skin around her lips.

"Sorry." Creed threw the tape down and pulled her close

again. He gently kissed her lips and whispered, "Are they too sore? I'll stay away."

"You might have to go easy on them for a day or two."

Creed shook his head. "I hate the duke even more right now."

Kiera smiled. "At least I don't have to worry about an upper lip wax anytime soon."

Creed chuckled and hugged her. "Oh, I love you."

"I love you." She rested her head in the crook of his neck and watched the men being arrested around them and the women being set free. The horror of the night swept over her, and she started trembling and couldn't stop.

Creed swayed with her slightly. "I'm here, love. Nobody's ever going to hurt you."

She glanced up at him. "You won't leave me again?"

He shook his head, more serious than she'd ever seen him. "Nothing on God's green Earth could ever take me away from you again."

Kiera arched up on tiptoes and kissed him. She didn't care that her lips were tender.

A throat cleared nearby, and they pulled apart and turned as one to focus on the James Bond guy.

"Sutton." Creed pulled one arm free and extended his hand. "Impeccable timing, old chap."

Sutton gave him a patient smile. "I'll show you who's the old chap, you chump."

Creed inclined his chin toward William's body. "Guess you got your wish for a bullet between his eyes."

Sutton shrugged. "Corbin claims he would've shot you." His smile became more genuine. "I'm not complaining." He inclined his chin to Kiera. "My apologies, Miss Richins, that things got so out of control. You took a bit of a swim?"

Kiera half-laughed, it came out as a gargle. This Sutton was the guy who had told Creed that she'd been living with Milo. She shouldn't like him, but it was hard to resist his charm and the obvious respect everyone around him showed to him. "I threw myself into the water to try to get away."

Creed's body shuddered against hers, and he pulled her in tighter. "Oh, love. You are so brave."

Kiera really did laugh then. "You guys are like superhuman warriors. I'm not brave at all."

Sutton tipped his head to them. "I'll leave you two alone to fight over who's bravest. I'll expect you in California next Monday, Creed."

"I quit, sir." Creed turned from Sutton and smiled down at Kiera.

Sutton arched an eyebrow. "I can respect that. Though I doubt you can stay away. I give you two weeks max. The door's open when you want back in."

"Thank you, sir."

Sutton nodded and walked away. Kiera focused on Creed's handsome face. "I don't even know what you do for James Bond. You quit so you won't have to leave me again?"

Creed nodded. "We do this." He gestured at his buddies who were either hauling men off, comforting the women who had almost been abducted, or joking with each other. "We protect and right wrongs and make the world a better place."

Kiera studied his handsome face and swallowed. "You know I want you around as much as possible, but I don't really want you sitting around all day watching me practice dancing."

Creed tilted his head and smiled. "What are you saying?"

"You were born to right wrongs, Creed. Maybe after a very long extended honeymoon, I might let you help this Sutton guy out a little more while I go back to performing on Broadway."

Creed shook his head before lifting her off of her feet and spinning her around. "I love you," he shouted.

The guys around them were chuckling. "Holy sappy sucker, keep it down." Someone called out.

"Shut it, Jace." Creed called back.

The guy just laughed in response. Another guy pulled out a pocket bible and a cross, giving them a life is good smile. "I can marry you here and now if you like."

Creed smiled. "Sounds good to me. What do you think? Shall we have Cannon marry us right here?"

Kiera shook her head, grinning. "I'd at least like to have a dry dress on."

Creed grinned, lowered her to her feet, and gently kissed her.

"My lips are actually feeling much better," she whispered.

Creed arched an eyebrow. "That's the best news I've heard all night." He pulled her against him and captured her lips with his own. Kiera melted into him, safety and love washing over her. They might not get married right this moment, but they would soon, and that was more than enough for her right now.

CHAPTER SIXTEEN

The next day dawned sunny and bright. Creed's friends had left sometime in the night, and it was only Kiera and Creed again. Just the way she liked it. They ate a late breakfast in her suite and then strolled along the beach, holding hands and savoring simply being together.

Creed suddenly turned to her and dropped down on one knee. "Kiera Richins. I haven't had time to talk to your father or get you a pretty ring, but I love you so much I can't stand it any longer. Will you marry me?"

Kiera grinned, staring down at his handsome face. This tough, military man, kneeling in the sand. "What did your friend call you last night? A sappy sucker?"

Creed chuckled and squeezed her hand. "Please don't make me wait any longer."

Kiera clung to his hand. "Of course I'll marry you, Creed."

He stood quickly and pulled her in tight, kissing her. It started out soft and lovely like a slow ballet, but then it crescendoed into a kiss that would give any salsa dance a run for its money. He pulled back, and they were both breathing hard. Leaning down, he rested his forehead against hers and whispered, "Can we elope today?"

Kiera laughed. Then she groaned, thinking of how wonderful it would be to elope and spend the next few weeks here with Creed. "Our mamas would kill us."

Creed studied her. "I can handle my mom. It's amazing how soft people go on you when you come back from the dead." He winked.

"You should be nicer to your mom, and I definitely can't disappoint my mama with an elopement. No matter how tempting you are." Kiera smiled and framed his face with her hands. "Christmas is only six weeks away. How about we fly our families down here for the holiday and get married right here on this beach?"

"Six weeks?" Creed looked pained. "I've been waiting my whole life to be married to you. I can't handle six more weeks."

Kiera laughed. "Wimp." She kissed him softly. "Think of what it will mean to our mamas to be part of it."

"You're right." Creed finally agreed. "I suppose I've put my mom through enough agony. It'll kill me, but I'll wait six weeks." He straightened and looked out over the beach. The dock where the battle had been last night was clearly visible. "Do you really want to get married here? I mean, after last night?"

Kiera smiled up at him. "This is where you and I reconnected. I'm not going to let some loser ruin the memories we've created here."

Creed grinned down at her. "Let's make some more good memories, just to make sure you have enough."

Kiera laughed, but he cut it off as he lifted her closer and kissed her until she was gasping for air. Lack of oxygen had never felt so beautiful.

THE HAWK BROTHERS

I hope you loved Creed and Kiera's story. If you missed the first Hawk brother's story about Emmett Hawk you can find it in *The Determined Groom*. I'm currently writing Callum Hawk's story, *My Billionaire Boss Fake Fiance*, which will be released November 6th. Bridger Hawk's story will be out near Christmas.

Hugs and thanks for reading,

Cami

ABOUT THE AUTHOR

Cami is a part-time author, part-time exercise consultant, part-time housekeeper, full-time wife, and overtime mother of four adorable boys. Sleep and relaxation are fond memories. She's never been happier.

Join Cami's VIP list and get a free copy of *Oh, Come On, Be Faithful* here.

You can also receive a free copy of *Rescued by Love: Park City Firefighter Romance* by clicking here and signing up for Cami's newsletter.

If you enjoyed *The Stealth Warrior* read on for an excerpt of *The Protective Warrior*.

cami@camichecketts.com
www.camicheckettts.com

THE PROTECTIVE WARRIOR

"This seat taken?" a nicely timbered voice asked.

Ally glanced up and took her time looking over him before she answered.

He arched an eyebrow and smiled. "Did I pass muster?"

"How do you do?"

He cocked his head to the side. "I'm good. You?"

Ally laughed. "I'm glad you're good, but 'how do you do' is more like 'hello.'"

"Hello." He smiled, and ooh, he was cute. "So I do pass muster?" He moved to sit down.

Ally held out a hand. "Not so quick, chump." His dark hair was short, military or missionary short, but it was nice—clean and thick and would probably feel good beneath her fingertips. His face was lean and proportioned with a firm jaw, a straight nose, and smooth, tanned skin. She liked the crinkles next to his eyes and mouth as he smiled at her, awaiting her perusal. He'd had some experiences in life, good and bad, if those crinkles told her anything. He was a big guy—broad and at least six-three with lots of lovely muscles peeking out from underneath his T-shirt and board shorts. It was his eyes that finally convinced her to accept his request. Their deep brown sparkled at her, though she could tell he could be very serious.

He tapped the edge of his tray. "How about now?"

"Okay, no harm in sharing a table." She grinned. "But I'm not keen on taking you home ... no matter how appealing those puppy-dog eyes are."

His eyebrows both went up at that. He set his tray down and slid into the seat. "Do you regularly take men home?"

"Don't get your hopes up." She winked at him and picked a bite of rib off the bone, savoring the tang of the barbecue sauce and the heartiness of the meat. No, she never took men home, only selectively dated those who passed her intuition test. She trusted her intuition completely and she could have fun with this hot, tough-looking guy.

He laughed and dug into his brisket. "Mm. This place is good."

"One of my favorites."

"Have you been on the island long?"

She wished. "A few days."

"Oh. You act like a local." He ate a bite of beans and took a drink of water before asking, "Which part of England are you from?"

"London. Kensington, to be exact. You?"

"Long Island originally. I like your accent a lot."

"I've been in the States for over six years, so it's faded."

"Don't let it fade."

That made her smile. "So, I'm Ally."

He nodded. "Pleasure to meet you."

"And you are?" He didn't seem to reveal much, but he was super attractive and was putting off good vibes. She prided herself on being able to read people, and this good-looking man had a great aura—confident and strong but mindful of others. Ally had no problem making a new friend.

"River."

"And what are your plans today, River?"

"Besides eating lunch with you?"

She smiled. "Yeah, besides that."

"I was hoping to go on a hike. You know any good ones?"

"For sure. Fancy a buddy?" She took a bite of the chunky chili.

"I'd love one."

"Let's do it." She took a long sip of water and appraised him. This day kept getting better and better. Picturesque scenery, beautiful weather, nice bike ride, yummy lunch, and now a fine-looking buddy to go on a hike with.

They finished lunch and walked toward the parking lot. "I need to run by my house to pick up my trainers and backpack," Ally said. "Do you want to meet up in half an hour?"

"Sure. Where?"

She gave him directions to the Nā Pali coastline hike trailhead and walked away. Turning back, she saw him watching and gave him a little wave. Yep, he was cute, yet he had a little bit of a bad-boy feel. She grinned to herself. Running away from home was definitely the best move she'd made.

Find *The Protective Warrior* here.

ALSO BY CAMI CHECKETTS

Navy Seal Romance

The Protective Warrior

The Captivating Warrior

Texas Titan Romance

The Fearless Groom

The Trustworthy Groom

The Beastly Groom

The Irresistible Groom

The Determined Groom

Billionaire Beach Romance

Caribbean Rescue

Cozumel Escape

Cancun Getaway

Trusting the Billionaire

How to Kiss a Billionaire

Onboard for Love

Shadows in the Curtain

Billionaire Bride Pact Romance

The Resilient One

The Feisty One

The Independent One

The Protective One

The Faithful One

The Daring One

Park City Firefighter Romance

Rescued by Love

Reluctant Rescue

Stone Cold Sparks

Echo Ridge Romance

Christmas Makeover

Last of the Gentlemen

My Best Man's Wedding

Change of Plans

Counterfeit Date

Snow Valley

Full Court Devotion: Christmas in Snow Valley

A Touch of Love: Summer in Snow Valley

Running from the Cowboy: Spring in Snow Valley

Light in Your Eyes: Winter in Snow Valley

Romancing the Singer: Return to Snow Valley

Other Books by Cami

Seeking Mr. Debonair: Jane Austen Pact

Seeking Mr. Dependable: Jane Austen Pact

Pass Interference: A Last Play Romance

Saving Sycamore Bay

How to Design Love

Oh, Come On, Be Faithful

Protect This

Blog This

Redeem This

The Broken Path

Dead Running

Dying to Run

Fourth of July

Love & Loss

Love & Lies

Cami's Collections

Billionaire Beach Romance Collection

Billionaire Bride Pact Collection

Billionaire Romance Sampler

Echo Ridge Romance Collection

Texas Titans Romance Collection

Made in the
USA
Middletown, DE

77279102R00086